THE DEAD LOOK ON

GERALD KERSH

THE DEAD
LOOK ON

A NOVEL

REYNAL & HITCHCOCK · NEW YORK

To

*The fighting spirit of all those who
live and hope for freedom.*

Contents

[vii]

CONTENTS

THE DEAD LOOK ON

I

Butcher, Butcher, Kill Ox!

"As long as iron can take a point, watch your backs!" Petz, clutching his cigar, stood in a ring of ashes. Dry, hot-eyed and dark, with his charred eye-sockets and his clipped gray hair and mustache which had the carbonized iridescence of coke, he seemed to have burned himself out in the night. Even his voice had a husky rasp, as of cinders. He said: "The trees grow cudgels: wear your helmets! String can strangle: mind your throats! While there is a roof for a stone to fall from, watch your step! As long as men have toes to creep on, sleep light! Beware of strange women, shadowy doorways, and quiet streets. Dark nights are dangerous: don't walk alone!"

He paused. Cigar-ash fell to the carpet. His hand must have been trembling: the smoke of his cigar rose straight for an inch or two and then fell into jerky coils before it spun itself into the stale gray veil that floated about the room. They had been smoking since midnight. Crushed cigarette-ends and burst cigar-butts filled the ashtrays. In Saxson's saucer there lay a stinking yellow soup of Turkish tobacco and spilled coffee, in which flakes of charred paper gradually disintegrated. Fingers had yellowed, eyes had reddened, chins had gone blue, cheeks had sagged, lips had cracked, tongues had furred. But still Bertsch sat, rosy and fresh, drawing on a blotting pad.

Bertsch had started by defining a square, almost geometrically exact. Then he produced the sides of the square, superimposed more squares; produced the sides of those, crammed squares within squares, breathlessly avoiding the coincidence of any two lines, meticulously dragging out a mazy, crazy pattern of straight lines. He was engrossed: the pattern seemed to enrage and fascinate him. He could not stop. There were always four lines left loose: he was compelled to go on and on, fitting square to square, faster and faster. He had been doing this for hours. They watched him. It meant that Bertsch was thinking.

Bertsch hummed under his breath. Petz concluded:

"*Slaven sind Sklaven*. Yes, Slavs are slaves. The Obergruppenfuehrer is right. Always right," he added, as Bertsch suddenly raised his big smooth face and looked at him. "Always right. But . . ."

"But exactly what?" asked Bertsch.

"We should take extraordinary precautions," said Petz.

"Colonel Petz, you are just a little bit tired," said Bertsch, very amiably; and Petz sat down as if he had been clubbed, and was silent.

"I agree——" said Saxson.

"Will you permit me to have the honor of saying a little word?" asked Bertsch. Saxson shut his mouth with a click.

Bertsch then said, lazily tearing up the spoiled blotting paper and smiling: "It seems quite clear. Time will kill this generation. We will assist Time. Excellent. *One:* we skim off the cream of the population and decant it; conscript the heavy labor. *Two:* the old people and the old memories will die of their own accord. *Three:* the children are ours. In ten years the Czechs are on their bellies. There is a new generation, bred to obedience. Famous! You can teach a child to say its prayers to you as to a Jesus Christ. Fine, fine! But that was not the point. The point was, subjugating this rabble at the present moment.

"Now if you have a lazy recruit in the Army, what do you do? Simply, you break him. You make it clear that life will not be worth living unless he does precisely what he's told. You make him see that his game isn't worth the candle. You give him merry hell until he screams for pity. If necessary, you kill him, as a salubrious example. He works or dies. Yes? Good.

"Now with a population, the same thing obtains."

Bertsch took out a cigarette. Petz, Saxson, and Breitbart all leaned forward with lighted matches. Bertsch took a light from Breitbart and went on:

"Nobody is alone. Every son of a dog has a pal, or a mistress, or a wife, or a child, or a brother, or a sister, or a father, mother, sweetheart—the devil knows what all. Whatever a man loves, that is his vulnerable spot, my friends. A man doesn't mind dying by himself: that's simple. But make it clear to him that his whole family are hostages, guarantors of his absolute obedience! You just make that clear and see the difference! He'll come to heel, then, and like it. Now I worked this out very logically in Bohdan. Remember Bohdan? There was some mumbling among the factory hands. Production was slow. They said they couldn't get the work done in the time. So one fine day I picked out one in every ten, haphazard, and hanged them. (I noticed, then, that one young fellow came forward and asked to be hanged in place of somebody or other who had a sick wife and six children. A man alone *enjoys* self-sacrifice!) Well, I hanged one in ten, and said to the

[4]

rest: 'Now can you get the work done in the time?'
Still they didn't. So I reduced them by another tenth.
And in short . . . Look: there were 550 hands there,
in the first place; they said they simply couldn't
manage the work in hand. But that same work got
done when I had strung up 200 of them. Get it? 350
men did the work that 550 couldn't do. And why?
Because I put the fear of God into them.

"Those 350 were all family men. I had 'em by the
short hair. I simply said to them: 'No comfortable
little hangings for you, my dears. But—you over
there!' and I called out a fellow called Prokop. I
said to him: 'Prokop, my friend, come here. You
support a mother, don't you? And a sister, don't
you?' I said. 'A nice sister, I think; a little, darkish
sister, nearly grown up? Now that, Prokop, is very,
very dutiful of you,' I said. And I grabbed him by
the collar, and I said: 'Now. Start something. Raise
one finger. Give one look. Say one word. I promise
on my word of honor as a German officer and a
gentleman that I won't do a thing to you. Not to
you, Prokop, my dear little friend. Well, do you
want to stop work?'

"He said: 'No, sir.'

"I said to him: 'You can run away if you like.
You won't be punished. Where would you like to
go? Say the word.' I said: 'Nothing will happen to
you, Prokop, my lad. But . . . that is a charming

[5]

little sister you have, Prokop, my dear friend. She is quite a pretty little girl, that sister of yours. And your mother . . . So charming, so sweet. Does she dance?'

"This Prokop said: 'No, sir.'

"I said: 'We might teach her to dance, on the end of a bit of telegraph wire, Prokop. Well, Prokop?'

"He said: 'Please, I want to go back to work, sir.'

"I said: 'I'm not sure that the Reich wants unwilling men to work for it. Are you willing, Prokop? Are you eager?'

" 'Yes, sir,' he said, and he was sweating like a Dutch cheese, 'I am willing and eager.'

" 'Beg, then,' I said. And he went down on his knees. So I gave him a good hiding and sent him back to work, him and his pals. And my God, did those dung-faces work! So remember the Bohdan Principle. Make it clear. Hang a family or two if necessary, without any regard for age or sex. Bear in mind that people are soft in their sentiments. They are always trying to protect somebody. I will stake my life on it, that within one year Czech resistance will be utterly and completely crushed. I am grateful for Colonel Petz's solicitude. Caution is always necessary. Even a rat will bite, if cornered. But even a rat will not try and break his teeth against an iron hand.

"Good. Good. The Order will be printed in a few

[6]

hours. There is no cause for uneasiness. The Slavs are in hand. It is now a kind of routine-matter of training. The fire is out. The teeth are drawn. The claws are filed. The collar is riveted. It is only a question of coördinating the whip-crack and the effort of the work-beast."

Everybody rose.

"Colonel Petz," said Bertsch, laying a kindly hand on the burned-up man's shoulder. "One secret of animal-breaking is, to walk with confidence. Eh?" He did not wait for a reply, but smiled and said: "You are tired, my poor friend. Take a rest. Rest for seven days. Find yourself some nice girls. Drink some wine. Relax, Petz, relax. I will send you to Berlin for a week."

Then, affably ignoring Petz's thanks, Bertsch went to the door. Saxson opened it for him. Outside, feet stamped. Heels snapped.

"Dawn," said Bertsch.

He stood on the top step between the rigid sentries. Breitbart, Saxson, and Petz stood beside him. It was marvelous to see how calm and fresh Bertsch looked, in contrast to the others. He looked down, breathing deeply. "Ah," he said, "it is good to breathe!" The sky was filling with a beautiful pale light. Driven by a remote wind, little pink downy clouds were floating away. Bertsch paraphrased Goethe: "Ah . . . if one could say to the passing moment: 'Stay a little—you are so beautiful!'"

At that moment a man passed, riding a motor-cycle. There was a stuttering bang and a thunder of acceleration. Sparrows rose, twittering; pigeons dropped and soared with a flapping of wings. "Stop that man," said Bertsch, and sat down on the top step. His face was blue. "He has shot me," he said; and then he began to cry out in a thin, high voice.

The whole town seemed to start up, wide awake and shouting. Sirens were screaming, and so was Bertsch. His screwed-up mouth looked no bigger than the finger-hole of an ocarina in his huge round face. There was only one bullet-wound in his body, just below the navel. Could one small bullet do so much to so vast a man? A doctor came, breathless. He filled a hypodermic syringe and emptied it into Bertsch's arm, which was bigger than a bolster. Bertsch subsided. More doctors came. Where had the bullet gone? A famous surgeon located it. It had broken Bertsch's spine. "It will take a miracle of God to save him," the surgeon said.

Cars rushed through the street. All the wires in the world were humming and jumping. Teleprinters and ticker-tapes clattered and clicked. . . . B . . . E . . . R . . . T . . . S . . . C . . . H . . . *Bertsch—Bertsch!—Bertsch—Bertsch!* gasped the express trains, touching ninety miles an hour down the gradients: *Murder-of-Bertsch! Murder-of-*

Bertsch! And the whistles screeched. Prague snapped at Berlin: Berlin roared at Prague. An army of detectives flew out. They combed the town like a head of hair, they turned the town inside out like a pocket, drew it like a fowl; skinned it alive. Airplanes hedge-hopped over the roads. The redness faded from the blue-gray morning. Another redness darkened on Bertsch's blue-gray tunic. A wild hue-and-cry whirled like a tornado round Bohemia and Moravia, picking up everything from church spires to grains of dust. 250,000 marks reward for the apprehension of the killer of Bertsch, Obergruppen-fuehrer and General of Police.

Killer? Yes. Limp and empty as his discarded trousers, he was dying. Only they would not let him die. Heinz Horner had flown in. Bertsch, looking up in his agony, could see Horner's face. "Let me die," he said; then, "Save me!" Horner replied: "Pull yourself together, try and think clearly. You can't die like this and leave loose ends of work. Come now, talk a little, Bertsch. Think. Your files concerning the Three Villages are not complete. Pull yourself together, Bertsch. Play the man! Give us some rough idea. . . ."

"The little red apples," said Bertsch.

"Little red apples," said Heinz Horner, taking notes.

"Yes? Like a chicken, like a coal mine! Dance,

dance, on nothing! With a telegraph wire, and the waves the waves. . . ."

Heinz Horner realized that Bertsch was delirious, and said: "Fat pig." He shook Bertsch's shoulder. Bertsch tried to bite him. One of the three greatest surgeons in the world said: "You are hurting him terribly." Horner shrugged his shoulders, and the anguish of Bertsch was such that even the little disturbance which the shrug made caused him to yelp like a dog.

"If you talk, Bertsch, you may have some morphia," said Horner. "Come. The Three Villages business! The Railroads Affair! The——"

"His name was Prokop," said Bertsch.

"Prokop."

Twelve hours later Bertsch died. Heinz Horner announced:—

"A reward of eight hundred thousand marks will be paid for information leading to the arrest of the murderer of Max Bertsch, S.S. Obergruppenfuehrer and General of Police."

Czechoslovakia became blank and flat, like a Slav face.

"Anybody sheltering or otherwise assisting the criminal, or withholding information likely to lead to his arrest, will be shot, together with his entire family, men, women, and children."

Czechoslovakia was silent.

To Petz, Heinz Horner said: "Bertsch mentioned a certain name, Prokop. Do you know any Prokop?"

"There must be tens of thousands of Prokops," said Petz.

"We have tens of thousands of rounds of ammunition," said Heinz Horner. He rolled a small, heavy object up and down the palm of his right hand. "A sub-machine-gun bullet," he said. "It comes out of Bertsch's belly. It tells us nothing. (How he yelled, eh?) And the man on the motorcycle; the light was dim, nobody saw his face. And the cycle itself. . . ."

"A heavy model, dark gray," said Petz.

"I know that much."

"I am checking on every motor——"

"So I should think, Colonel Petz. And every recently repainted one. And every tuned-up one. And every man capable of riding one. And every man who seems to be going somewhere in a hurry. And all the rest of it. That is routine work. Well, go away now, and let me think."

Heinz Horner sat and thought. He thought best on weak tea. Horner was a thorough man, ambitious, precise, esteemed for his nerveless cunning and his cold inquisitiveness, his dogged obstinacy and his pitiless energy. You would never have noticed him in a group of ordinary men. There was primness in the shape and set of his rimless spectacles on his nondescript nose; modesty in the cut of his small

black mustache. The normal worries of a family
man might have cut the wrinkles in his forehead and
made his hair recede. He looked less than life-size,
and had that about him which suggested the shabby-
gentility of a village schoolmaster who is secure in
a regulated mediocrity yet always a little harassed:
the same staid manner, air of petty authority, and
scornfully explanatory tone. Several years before, a
Social-Democrat journalist had written: *Hans An-
dersen might have told a department store fairy-tale
about the papier-maché passion of a dressmaker's
headless dummy stuck with pins, and a figure for the
display of shoddy stock-size business suits . . .
How, at last, they married, and, in a bed marked
STYLISH: GREAT BARGAIN, produced a drab
doll that walked and talked but had no heart . . .*
The journalist hanged himself in Dachau in 1934;
but he had put into words what many people
thought about Horner.

Dull, colorless, plain, passionless, Heinz Horner
sipped his tea and sat stiffly in the dead man's chair.
Far beyond earshot, men walked on tiptoe and spoke
in whispers. Once, Horner sneezed: it sounded like
the sweep of a scythe. Once, he smiled, and when he
smiled his face changed. It looked like a respectable
room in which some crime has been committed. His
eyes wrinkled; his spectacles became, somehow, dim
and frightening, like windows in a deserted house in

which, in the dead of night, a light begins to flicker
. . . somebody dangerous is hiding there. There was
something burning behind those eyes that should not
have been burning. And when Heinz Horner laughed
his throat clicked—you thought of the ticking of a
dark clock in a silent passage.

Late that night a messenger came. Near a little
village on a little river an abandoned motorcycle
had been found.

The name of this village was Dudicka.

Like a man who crushes an insect, Heinz Horner
stabbed his thumb at a black button. Something
buzzed like a wasp. Petz came in.

"Dudicka," said Horner. "Population?"

* * * *

The population of Dudicka had increased by two
that night. The wife of Roman Kafka had given
birth to twins; now, four hundred and five people
lived in the village. It was a small place, packed into
the dog-leg bend of the Dudicka Stream: ninety little square houses and a church. The runaway junk-
barrow of history had shaken out one or two curi-
osities in Dudicka; cracked and questionable shards
of an uncertifiable past. It was said that blind King
John of Bohemia had passed through Dudicka; only
he was not blind then, for he said: "How calm, how
beautiful," and sent for a girl who happened to take

his fancy. There might be royal blood in the village. Furthermore, Ziska, whose skin was made into a drum, slept one night in Dudicka, and blessed the place. It is quite certain that the Liberator Masaryk visited Dudicka, and loved to walk among its walnut trees; several of the villagers had seen him—a fine old man with a certain sublime calm and eyes deep and clear as peaceful water, who was one of them and all of them.

In Dudicka, the Balaban family had made glass for nearly two hundred and fifty years. The Balabans were still there. Jan Balaban and his two sons, working with obsolete tools, still blew flasks and goblets delicate and strong as bubbles. You could tell a Balaban glass in the dark: it rang with a sob, making a lingering melancholy music. A Hungarian nobleman—an Esterhazy—looking into one of Balaban's limpid cups and ringing it with his finger, said: "You must have made this glass of tears." That was in 1800. The phrase caught: *Tear-glass*. A Dresden manufacturer offered old Jan Balaban a little fortune for the secret of it. "There is no secret," he said. The manufacturer analyzed a Balaban cup. It was glass; fine glass, but only glass. "It is in our breath," said Balaban. "Ink is only ink, a pen is only a pen, paper is only paper: it is the voice of God that makes the Word. Glass is only glass, sir: the rest is in the breath and the wrist, and the eye." His own eyes were red with inflammation. The Dresdener said: "Fifty thousand marks—not a pfennig more." "There is no secret that I know," said Balaban. The manufacturer went away and made a line of high-priced glasses that looked like Balaban's: but nothing would make them sob. So Balaban grew old and poor: his sons grew up, fine craftsmen, heavy men with light hands. But something was lost. Had something gone out of the raw material? Or the wood that made the charcoal? The Balabans could blow a glass as clear as a star and more graceful than a flower; but when you rang it there were no tears in it, only a wavering sigh behind the fine clanging note.

Karel Marek, the schoolmaster, had once written a story which was printed in a newspaper. In substance, the story was as follows: A man, having inherited some money, spent a whole day in the town, buying things. On his way home he fell in with a strange traveler of chilling aspect, muffled in a great black cloak. The man began to talk, boasting of his good fortune and showing his purchases to the stranger in the black cloak. "This suit of clothes is warranted to last ten years. . . . These boots are guaranteed to wear for twenty years. . . . This watch is certified for half a century. . . . This hat will last a lifetime. . . . I have twelve shirts of the strongest and finest linen . . . and I am laying down a cellar full of wine that will be worth a fortune in fifteen or twenty years from now. Am I not fortunate above all other men? I, Oleg Petera?" The stranger in the dark cloak said: "Oleg Petera, yes: I have been waiting for you since this morning." Petera said: "And who are you?" And the stranger in the black cloak replied, in a voice of infinite pity: "I am the Angel of Death."

It was printed, with a picture. Karel Marek wrote hundreds more such stories, but no newspaper would look at them, and so they collected dust in his cupboard.

Otakar Blazek, the butcher, made a kind of sausage that was famous throughout the district. Another Blazek, Josef, kept the inn at Dudicka. Roman Kafka owned the tobacco shop. Two men who had been boys in Dudicka were lawyers in Prague. There had been only one crime committed in Dudicka since the beginning of the century—the man who owned the store, one Vojtech, had got horribly drunk and tried to strangle his wife: his eldest son stabbed him with a knife.

For the rest, Dudicka lived on its orchards, its walnut trees, its pigs and its forest. It had a quarry, out of the debris of which the schoolmaster had picked a collection of fossils. Of this, the priest had said: "Little reptiles, little fishes, insects—even weeds and grasses—not a leaf lives and dies but its life and death is recorded."

Dudicka had a mayor and a village idiot; a richest man and a poorest man; a petty miser and a petty spendthrift; good girls, bad girls, faithful wives, unfaithful wives, dutiful sons, wild sons; one or two saints and one or two mischief-makers; idle men, laborious men. They were people, like other people. They wanted to live between the extremes. They had known good times and bad. Dudicka was a place like ten thousand other places.

* * * *

Heinz Horner put down his tea glass. Petz and Saxson looked over his shoulder at the map spread out before him. Horner was holding a big blunt black pencil: the shiny graphite looked moist in the light, like the nose of a hunting-dog. It nuzzled, quivered a little, pointed; followed a river, sped up a tributary, paused, darted away again up a little bent stream, and stopped.

Delicately, with two fingers of his left hand, Horner pressed two buttons, a black one and a white one. Two buzzers, high-pitched and low, vibrated in a horrible discord.

Petz looked at Saxson: Saxson looked at Petz.

"Day will break in two hours' time," said Horner.

Very neatly he drew a ring round the village called Dudicka. Men were running. "To work," said Heinz Horner.

II

The Miraculous Shower of Flowers

A VERY WONDERFUL THING happened at dawn in
Dudicka. Two people declared their love for each
other, and as they did so the sky blossomed like an
apple tree in a beautiful profusion of drifting pink
flowers.

The boy was Max Marek, and the girl's name was
Anna Horak. They had spent most of their child-
hood together, in the house of Karel Marek, the
schoolmaster. Max was his nephew. He had the un-
mistakable Marek face—an odd, arresting face, ugly
and amiable, of a peculiar but not a wrong shape. It
was one of those strange Slovak blends that must be
considered as a whole. The features, individually
awkward, combined to form something harmonious
and indescribably pleasant. The heavy, thoughtful
expression was appropriate to it, as clouds are appropriate to certain rocky landscapes. A sneer or a

wink would have disfigured it like a bomb-splinter:
it was designed to express nothing but decent emo-
tion—and that only in moderation. His light gray
eyes were always wide open, like the account-books
of an honest tradesman. An unseemly word coming
out of that plain, firm mouth, would have made you
pinch yourself and wonder whether you were dreaming: it would have horrified you by its wild improb-
ability—as if he had shot out a forked tongue and
hissed. This was a sound man, solidly constructed of
good stuff; shaped like a peasant but dressed like a
decent townsman in a suit of dull gray cloth that was
chosen because it was likely to last and would not
show the dust. He had to be careful, spend pru-
dently, make a shirt last a week and a suit last a
year in everyday use; think twice before riding on
a tram; fill out little meals with bread; write small
to save paper, and get as many shaves as possible
out of a razor blade.

In Prague, where he was studying medicine, he
shared an attic hardly bigger than a dog-kennel with
a law student as poor as himself. He made secret
notes of all the money his Uncle Karel gave him: in
another three years he would be a doctor. Then he
would specialize in nerves, do great work, make a lot
of money, and overwhelm the old man with gifts.
Who took him in, an orphan, and brought him up
with love and tenderness, and sent him to the Uni-

versity? Uncle Karel. Sometimes, Max permitted himself certain fantasies: One day he would steal all Karel's stories out of the cupboard, and send them to a publisher, and pay for their publication in a beautiful binding. Then one day later, Uncle Karel would receive a parcel: a dozen presentation copies of the Collected Stories of Karel Marek. . . .

But first, qualify. He worked with a kind of frenzied patience; studied in the manner of the serious-minded student, pinning lists of terms and carefully-drawn diagrams on the tiny walls of his attic; passed examinations; dreamed dreams of unprecedented scientific discoveries and acts of gratitude (which was his way of relaxing); developed a faculty for concentrated study. He worked with doggedness and intuition. In spite of his self-contained, single-minded devotion to work, he was well-liked. His big hands, which a thousand years of hard gripping had shaped, had a strange delicacy in their touch: they could feel their way. He could tear a telephone directory in two, or pick up a cigarette-ash without breaking it. His mind was like that, also. He had a strength, a delicacy, and a frankness that commanded respect. And he was generous with everything that he regarded as his to give away—his capacity for clear and simple explanation, and such time as he permitted himself for rest and amusement. Max had no enemies, and had never disliked anybody in his life; except one person, a girl.

So here is a strange thing. The girl he had disliked was Anna Horak.

Their association had begun with a fight. Anna was five: Max was six. Anna's father was Vojtech Horak—the man whose son stabbed him because he got drunk and beat his mother. One hot puff of red violence seemed to destroy the Horak family as fire destroys dry grass. Vojtech Horak died. The son, Josef, went to prison, and died. The mother took to her bed, and died. Anna was left alone. Karel Marek, a middle-aged bachelor then, had taken her into his house and adopted her: a little girl for him, and a playmate for little Max. That was sixteen years before. Anna was an unprepossessing child, with a flat face, lank hair, and little eyes. Her forehead was low, her shoulders were high; her limbs were too small, her mouth was too large; her brows descended, her nose turned up; her speech was slow, her temper was quick, and she shunned company.

Karel Marek was as gentle as her mother had been, but he was also strong. Anna had lived her five years in an indeterminate atmosphere of violence and abject apology and promises made to be broken. The calm of Karel Marek, the schoolmaster, shook her: she disliked it at first. And she suspected the affable overtures of Max . . . A smile, to her, was a disarming preliminary to a blow: if the other person is of your own size, hit him first—that was the basic principle. She fought with Max for years. Then she became a sister to him. He went away to school, and when he came back things had changed. Some magic had been worked. Max had begun to set firm. He was more than a boy: he was masculine, thickset, grave, wise, poised. His hair—which had been merely hair—was now brown hair.

Anna, also, had come under some strange influence. She had grown upwards and outwards. Her eyes were large. Her mouth was still large, but there was more face around it; and her hair was no longer lank, but straight and exceedingly black: she had large breasts and a certain odor.

They treated each other with punctilious courtesy. There was a restraint between them. They had nothing to talk about. She wished he would go away. He found that she made him indefinably uneasy, and, disliking her all the more, became coldly polite.

Now, his studies being interrupted, he had come home again for a little while. Formidable forces had been at work. They were strangers. Anna was a calm, slightly-smiling housekeeper: she moved gracefully, dressed her dense black hair in a heavy knot, and seemed to glow. Max observed that she had a skin like something smoldering under ivory, and a deep voice—whereas, before, she had simply

[22]

had a skin and a voice. Anna noticed that Max had square hands of a certain characteristic power, and that he had not grown a mustache: she suddenly felt that it was a good thing for Max, not to have grown a mustache.

They had nothing to say to each other, as before. Nevertheless they were conscious of each other's eyes. They found it embarrassing to look at each other. When they did so, neither of them wanted to be the first to look away: they were conscious of that, too. Then Max avoided Anna and Anna avoided Max. All the same, they met, by accident, in the unlikeliest places. Once, Anna asked him about girl-friends, speaking in an impersonal tone, but adding a queer laugh to round it off. She thought it was a nonchalant laugh. Max, for no reason at all, found himself saying, with unreasonable vehemence: "I spend all my time working. *All* my time, *all* of it. Absolutely all of it."

Anna said that she liked, sometimes, to go out at dawn; she liked the woods at dawn; she did not sleep very heavily, and always awoke at sunrise. Everything was so quiet; everything had such a sweet smell. "Too early for me," said Max, with false heartiness. But he awoke an hour before dawn, on this memorable day; arose and dressed as if he had to go somewhere in a great hurry and was afraid of being late.

[23]

What for? He did not ask himself what for. He went and looked at the chickens. From time to time he looked towards the house, with its strong square walls and its pointed roof. The sky was beginning to lighten. Where there had been moonlight, there was a different kind of light. Something moved behind the panes of Anna's window: there was an upward heave—somebody was taking off a garment. His heart thudded and his eyes shifted out of focus. He wanted to look again, but dared not. Two minutes passed; he heard nothing but a thumping in his ears, although birds had begun to sing and a cock was crowing. He looked away from the house, and saw the mâquis of very young trees that surrounded Dudicka; and the dark forest beyond. It occurred to Max that if he had one he would light a cigarette; this would give him something to do: but he had no cigarettes.

He turned. Anna was putting up her hair. He saw her standing at her little mirror. A jagged bit of early light had got caught in her hair: she was black-and-white in that light—black head, white body, black armpits, then black shadow. Max picked a blade of grass and began to eat it. He shook himself and walked away. But then he heard a door open quietly: he had good ears. Anna came out. All the birds in the world burst with music and splashed a million songs over the cool dawn.

Max stood very still. Anna walked towards him. Without knowing exactly what he was doing, he held out his hands. She smiled, and took them. In a deep, firm, serious voice, he said: "Anna. I love you very much."

"I love you very much too, Max," she said.

Then they kissed each other, and the dawn broke. Two large clear tears clung to Anna's eyelashes for a moment, and then dropped. A part of one tear—perhaps a quarter of a tear—hung on a corner of her lip. She licked it away, and said:

"I love you very much. I love you very, very much. I love you."

Max replied: "Yes. I love you."

He was holding his voice like a restive horse. He said: "I am going to marry you, Anna."

Anna answered: "Yes, you are going to marry me."

Something droned. She looked up into the sky, already dotted with birds.

"Look," she said.

Something in the sky had caught the light. Somewhere the day was breaking red; but they could not see that yet. A long way away, much higher than the birds, a rose-colored corolla broke open. It drifted in the upper air. It was so beautiful, so like a flower, that Max expected it to disintegrate in a fluttering shower of petals.

"Flowers," said Anna.

A second flower blossomed; then three more; then fifty; then a hundred. They hung, and floated down.

Anna said: "God knows I love you, and so he is throwing down flowers."

She felt Max's arm grow hard. Then he said:

"God knows I love you, too. But they are not flowers. They are parachutes." Inside him, something seemed to break loose and crash from side to side like a loosened cannon in a tossing ship. It was his heart.

III

Windfall of Poisonous Fruit

To ANNA, in the enchanted distance, Sergeant Schlager had looked like a flower. But to Sergeant Schlager, two seconds before, Dudicka had appeared, first, like some condemned symbolist painting . . . a bit of black in the shape of spilled ink, and a crescent of green plush. Within the crescent, a meaningless group of unconnected fragments—a spoonful of green-and-white diced turnips thrown down between a bit of bent wire and a strip of adhesive tape: a senseless and ugly combination of things.

They are not flowers, they are parachutes: Anna recognized them, then, and froze.

There is Dudicka! Sergeant Schlager felt something inside him coiling like a spring, and he knew that the blackness was the forest, the green plush was the mâquis, the iron wire was the Dudicka

Stream, and the diced carrots were little houses and gardens. As for the tape, that was the road.

Dudicka, the unknown village, was in a way honored by the presence of Schlager, who was an international celebrity. He had been a national idol when Hitler and Göring were still writhing in the muck-heap dropped by the First World War; when they were still pallid maggots, Schlager had grown colored wings. Even now there were thousands of people who knew nothing of Hitler except that he was a Leader, but who could describe, with a fanatical exactitude, the career of Sergeant Schlager. He was a big man with a fierce face and oblong brown eyes as quick and restless as cockroaches. Heavy-handed and light-footed, he had come punching out of the Hamburg gutters in the nineteen-twenties; clubbed down three heavyweights. Goebbels, sharp and accurate as a scavenger's spiked stick in picking up useful rubbish, portrayed him as a German knight-errant, a hammer-handed Aryan fighting-man. Goebbels put him into the parachute-troops. Here were men of courage, of initiative and iron discipline: this was the ideal place for a man like Heinie Schlager. Nazi youth followed him: he became a Sergeant, and his celebrity burned bright like a turned-up wick.

Heinz Horner sent him to Dudicka.

He came over, saw the place, and felt that sensa-

[28]

tion as of a wound-up spring between his heart and his stomach. Then, when the signal was given, he jumped. He was the first to jump. As his parachute opened, Anna cried "Look!" Schlager, also, cried out: not loud; it was more a grunt than a cry, as the harness jolted him when the cords slapped taut. He saw the crazy still-life beneath him spinning like a wheel in a black-and-green blur. Then it shook itself to a standstill and rushed up at him. The black became fleecy. Green stippled it—light was striking the tree-tops. The plushy green broke up, became blotchy. They were houses, the little white cubes. Sergeant Schlager clutched his machine carbine.

The adhesive tape stretched like rubber, darkened, and became a road: it swung up at him like the blade of a bat. He braced himself for the shock of landing; struck the road with a jolt that made his head tingle, and found himself on one knee in the dust. He threw off his parachute and stood up, a powerful and impressive figure with a stern face and gleaming eyes. Others were landing, with thuds and flutters.

"Follow me," said Sergeant Schlager.

They went into the village.

*   *   *   *   *

Otakar Blazek, the butcher, had a habit of waking

up before dawn. An hour before sunrise, at any time
of the year, his eyes snapped up like spring-blinds
and he was wide awake. Now, there was nothing for
him to do. But he still awoke at the same time and
loitered, disorientated, wavering like a broken com-
pass. At fifty-five Blazek had no possessions but a
bare house, a few tools, and an old dog. Time and
war had blown the Blazeks away. Of all his family,
only his father was still alive, but it would have been
better for the old man if he had died several years
ago, for he was quite deaf, almost blind, and too
weak to move. Otakar had no means of making him
understand what had happened to Dudicka. Old
Blazek lived in a gray dream, in a twilight out of
which he crept once or twice a week to ask for impossible things—eggs, meat, wine, sausage. Before
the Germans had taken everything, Otakar had hidden in a secret place a few of the big Blazek sausages, fine dark sausages each as thick as a man's
forearm. The old man ate a slice or two every day:
the warm, spicy flavor of the sausage meant more to
him than meat. As if it had been a song or a motto,
it kept alive in him a certain will, a ghostly pride:
by virtue of this flavor he was different from other
men. Anybody in three parishes who tasted it would
say: "Blazek!"

But Otakar, sitting miserably on the edge of his
bed, thought: "If there is enough left to last the old

one two more weeks, what good will it do? It only drags things out. It makes worry. When the sausage is gone, what? Where is meat? In Hitler's belly. Where are spices? In India. There will be no more sausage. The old one cannot understand. The years have bent him round to where he started. Yes, God has cracked him like a pot."

He stood up. At the other side of the room something wheezed like the springs of an old sofa. Then something scratched, clicked and scuffled on long-nailed paws, breathing with the melancholy twang of a broken mouth organ. It was the dog, Hektor. Hektor, also, had an invariable morning routine: he came to be kicked. It had begun when Hektor, as a pup of idiotic appearance, had come lolloping over the floor to lick his master's boot: Otakar, impelled by sheer force of habit, had kicked him across the room like a ball; but Hektor chose to accept this as a caress, a little game. Panting with delighted anticipation, he had run up for his morning kick every morning for twelve years. Once, Otakar was ill, and stayed in bed for three days. Hektor pined. On the fourth day Otakar arose and kicked the dog three times; that was the happiest morning of Hektor's long, happy life.

He was a powerful, stupid dog of grotesque shape. In sixty generations he must have had a hundred and twenty different ancestors—and one of these, it was said, must have been a man, for there was something fantastically human in the shape and expression of his face, in spite of the great flat snake-like skull and the ragged, bat-like ears. He had the chest of a mastiff, the forelegs of a bulldog, the loins of a wolfhound, the rump of a Dobermann-Pinscher; a tail no larger than a man's thumb and curved upward like the spout of a coffeepot. His smooth hide was scarred in a hundred places. He had fought many deadly battles: time had been when he could flash fangs like a panther's, and had the pulling-power of a mule. Now, he was very old and covered with fat: twelve years is a great age for a dog.

"Hektor!" said Otakar.

The dog reached his master. The ponderous kick slammed into Hektor's ribs: he slid across the floor on his long nails like a heavy table on casters, and came back panting with ecstasy.

"You too," said Otakar. Now that he was lonely he often talked to the dog. "Look at you. Black shame! You are old, you stink, you are no good to yourself, and there's nothing for you to eat. All you get is a kick in the belly. Every day you get slower and sleep more. It's about time I finished you off: it'd be a kindness. Yes, Hektor, it'd be a kind thing to do you in."

In Otakar's tone there was a solemnity, a sadness which Hektor understood. He stopped grinning and lowered himself clumsily to the floor, lying so that the soft underpart of his jaw fitted over the toecap of Otakar's nearest boot.

"I can't feed you. I can't feed myself. There is only a bit of sausage for the old man—only a taste of it. And so what are you to do? Answer me, what are you to do?"

The dog was silent.

"They took away my gun, or I'd shoot you. Can I knock you on the head? I could open you a vein, but God help you, you are so fat. I don't know where your veins are, and I don't want to hurt you very much. But you can't go on, your time's up. But what a dog you were! What a devil! Another day, another week, what difference? . . . Only I don't mind telling you, I can't say I like to do it to you."

Hektor whined breathily: it was like the swish of a cane.

"Here comes another day."

Dawn broke.

Otakar went to the door. "I don't mind telling you I've had just about enough of it myself," he said, in a low voice. Hektor waddled after him into the yard. "Well, I don't mind telling you . . . I never took another wife, and I won't have another dog. And this thing here—you've seen me use a poleax before, Hektor. It wasn't often I had to hit twice. And you see for yourself, I'm treating you right. I'm treating you like a bull, with a poleax; not like a pig or a sheep, with a sticker. You see that, Hektor. And if I had a gun I'd shoot you properly, as if you were a man. You know that."

Hektor whined. He knew that something awful was about to happen. Otakar stood over him with the poleax. But where was the beast? There was no beast. There was only the man, and himself, the dog.

Otakar held out his hand. Hektor licked it. "Now, Hektor, stand still!"

The poleax swung up. Hektor lunged forward with a rattling bark. Otakar turned on his heel. The yard door swung in, quivering.

Huge-shouldered, close-helmeted, booted to the knees and clutching a Schmeisser in one colossal fist, Sergeant Schlager strode in. Three soldiers followed him.

Hektor snarled.

"What are you doing?" asked Sergeant Schlager.

"Me?"

"You."

"I am killing my dog."

"What is your name?"

"Otakar Blazek."

"If you lie you will be shot. Who else lives here?"

This question was never answered. The dog Hektor uttered a noise like the breaking of a rusty bell, and, with one absurd but magnificent scrambling leap, hurled himself at Sergeant Schlager.

The Sergeant, as Heinie Schlager, might be contender for the heavyweight championship of the world. Heinie Schlager, as the Nazi with the Schmeisser, might be contender for the kingdoms of all the earth. Hektor knew only one thing: he had an air of menace, and was an intruder in Blazek's back yard; so he sprang at Schlager's throat. His old legs carried his old body about halfway up. Schlager's experienced left arm fended him off. An arm was not a throat, but it was better than nothing: Hektor seized it and held on. He tasted rubber and cloth; bit with all his might. This, this was the meaning of the strange solemnity of the morning! Hektor knew that he must never let go.

"Call this dog off!" cried Sergeant Schlager.

Otakar said nothing. Hektor's broken teeth had got through the cloth of the sleeve. He made a desperate effort to bite as he had bitten in the beginning of everything, when teeth cracked bones and eyes saw clear and life was joy. There was something hot in his head, like a log fire crackling and shooting out sparks. Crack!—sparks were flying out of his eyes.

Sergeant Schlager was hitting him on the head with the barrel of his carbine.

Hektor bit deeper, letting his great weight drag. Schlager, taking careful aim, struck once more. He could still knock out most men with his four-inch jab, if only they kept still enough to let him land it. Hektor was still: he wanted to get his teeth into that bone-hard arm. His eyes were red: he was set to hang there until he dropped off dead like fruit from a branch. The blow fell. The crackling log in Hektor's head blazed white, burst, and went black. Otakar heard the ring of metal and the absolute finality of the crunch that went with it.

Sergeant Schlager shook his arm and Hektor fell. The dog lay on his side. One of his hind legs quivered.

Otakar Blazek shouted: *"My* dog!" and rushed forward swinging his big red fists. He was one of the strongest men in Dudicka, and looked it. The soldiers behind Schlager grinned: this was going to be good. Sergeant Schlager shifted his machine carbine from his right hand to his left, said Hep! and hit Otakar in the jaw. The butcher fell with a heavy slap, as if he had dropped from a high window. "That, gentlemen, is what is known as a right hook," said Schlager, grinning.

A big blond man behind him said: "My God, I'd just as soon be kicked in the face by a cow as take a punch like that." He was a Westphalian peasant. Schlager smiled. But Blazek was getting up. His face was terrible. He had fallen an ox: he was rising a wild bull. He snatched the poleax and swung it back. Schlager danced back on one foot, found a grip on the Schmeisser carbine, and fired. He was still thinking in terms of knockout punches—in this case, a left to the heart and a right to the jaw—and his hands moved accordingly. It was an awkward, V-shaped burst; but there were ten shots in it, and Blazek was only four feet away. Six bullets hit him in the chest: he fell again, more heavily than before, and the poleax flew twinkling over his head and smashed a window behind him.

"I'd rather be poked in the ribs by me than by Brother Schmeisser," said Schlager to the blond man, and everybody laughed. "Now—into the house."

In the dust of the yard Hektor's hind leg stretched itself out in one last tremor. For one crazy instant you might have thought that this faintly-quivering dog's-leg was shaking the earth . . . for gently, but distinctly, the ground was shivering. But what you would have felt, actually, was the vibration of engines.

Down the road towards Dudicka rushed a thundering column of armed motorcyclists, followed by great armored cars and massive lorries. Behind the lorries purred a superb Mercedes-Benz escorted by half-a-hundred picked fighting-men on motorcycles, and followed by six mighty armored trucks. Over them all, small aircraft circled.

The noise of Schlager's Schmeisser-burst had flapped, shuddered and reverberated, echoing through Dudicka and the surrounding countryside, beating up clouds of terrified birds like dust from a shaken rug. Anna and Max, looking at each other, said—with one impulse—"Whatever happens, I love you."

"We said the same thing together," said Anna, holding out a crooked little finger. "Wish." They linked fingers and were silent.

Karel Marek, the schoolmaster, came out into the garden, tucking in his shirt. He said: "Did you hear?"

"It was a machine gun, Uncle Karel," said Max.

"Does this mean trouble, Father?" asked Anna.

The schoolmaster replied, very coolly: "No. It means Doom."

IV

The Ring That Horner Drew

Yᴇѕ, Dᴏᴏᴍ. Horner had pronounced it: in his mind the fate of Dudicka was cut like a steel die, unalterable, like a natural law. The sun and the Reich must rise: darkness and Dudicka must fall.

The journalist who hanged himself in Dachau had written:

Heinz Horner is the zealous official taken to his logical—and therefore nightmarish—conclusion. To achieve their effects Hitler and Göring must scream like mad horses in a fire. Horner rarely raises his voice above a dry monotone like the rustle of government blue paper. To him, everything is predestined by regulations. Human beings, to him, are cards in a steel cabinet: some he puts here, some he puts there, and some he tears up. He can kill a thousand men, or one man, with equal passionlessness. Imagine a calculating-machine into the rods

[39]

*and wheels of which have slipped certain inspira-
tions and instincts . . . some fantasy of Satan and
the conveyor-belt. This is Horner. Picture something disgusting—that this calculating-machine
needs your blood, and is ticking out permutations
and combinations of all the ways and means of getting it. You may be a man or a multitude: Horner
merely shifts a gear and ticks on, dreadfully accurate but horribly wrong; ticking, ticking, ticking towards the end he himself ordains.*

Doom? Worse: mathematics.

Horner was riding in the black Mercedes-Benz.

*   *   *   *   *

The Schmeisser-fire that cut Blazek down shook
the Mayor of Dudicka out of a heavy, clinging sleep.
He opened his eyes and saw that his wife was sitting
up, listening.

The Mayor, Mr. Hoza, was a fat and somnolent
old man. White flesh had blurred his chunky body
as fungi soften the outlines of a tree-stump. After
sixty-seven hard years he loved to luxuriate in bed,
lying between heaven and earth on a cloud of goose-
feathers, half-asleep and half-awake until nearly
seven o'clock. He had a smooth pink forehead like
cut ham, white eyebrows like trimmings of fat, and
a kind of Masonic insignia of right-angled white
mustache and triangular beard.

"What is it?" he asked.

"Somebody is shooting," his wife replied.

"Oh, of course," said Mr. Hoza; then sat up and shouted: "What? Shooting? Who, shooting? Shooting what? Where, shooting?"

Mrs. Hoza was a keen-eyed woman with a quick brain and sharp senses, ponderous and calm as an old mare, but alert as a voltmeter. "It sounded as if it came from near Blazek's," she said. "Airplanes have been coming over for half an hour."

"Well? Nowadays there are always airplanes."

"These were right overhead."

"Where else should they be? In the cellar?"

Then somebody knocked at the outer door, and a voice roared: "Open!" Hoza heard his daughter running down. He rolled out of bed and pulled on his trousers and boots. A latch clicked and a hinge squealed. The voice boomed in the house: "Jan Hoza, the Mayor, at once!" An officer's heels snapped on the floor, followed by heavy, thudding rubber soles. Smoothing his mustaches, Hoza went down. A captain of parachute-troops was in the house. Helmeted soldiers stood behind him.

"Yes?" said Hoza.

"Heil Hitler."

"Ah . . . Heil Hitler. What can I do for you?"

The Captain was a thin, hard man with a thin hard voice. "Hoza? Mayor of Dudicka?"

"Yes."

"You're under arrest."

"Why?"

"You'll find out. Who lives here with you?"

"My wife and my daughter and her child, my grandson." Mrs. Hoza came and stood behind her husband. The young woman, plump-faced and light-haired, waited. Her left hand held a shawl at her breast: a snub-nosed boy with a freckled nose came down and held her right hand. The Captain looked at the young woman. She was pregnant.

"You're under arrest, too, all of you. You—where's your husband?"

She answered: "Dead."

"Name?"

"His name was Josef Hertl."

"You lost no time, I see," said the officer, smiling.

"I beg pardon?"

He pointed. She flushed dark red and replied: "He has been dead five months only. I am a decent woman."

In her heavy, level voice, Mrs. Hoza asked: "What have we done now?"

"You are under arrest," said the Captain.

"But for what?"

"You are under arrest. You will not leave this house."

The old woman turned to Hoza and said: "My

man, mark my words—we are near the end of things."

Hoza stared at her. She added: "They do not need to drop people from airplanes to tell us that we are under arrest." And she smiled at the German officer. He simply said:

"Is this the Town Hall, so to speak?"

"Yes," said Hoza. Looking out of the window he saw the street was full of soldiers. "Listen," he said. "I am the Mayor and I have a right to know—what is happening here?"

"Oh. You are the Mayor. So you have a right to know. You want to know what is happening?"

"Please."

The Captain seemed to purr like a cat. "Then I'll tell you," he said. "*Things* are happening. Now: the register. Every man, woman, and child in this village."

A sergeant-major said to Mrs. Hoza: "If you——"

The Captain snapped at his sentence like a ferret at a rabbit: "*Feldwebel!*"

"Pardon me, Captain."

The Captain said: "Now, Mayor Hoza . . ."

"May I get dressed?" Hoza asked.

"No. You have my permission to be informal." The Captain smiled again. There were three sword-cuts on his right cheek. "Have you an office?"

"I keep my papers in the sitting room."

"Be so kind as to address me properly."

"Captain."

"Thanks." The Captain bowed very low, grinning. Then he straightened himself with a jerk, and, spitting out a little breath in the kind of chirping whistle one uses to call a dog, jerked a thumb. Hoza's forehead was white now. He opened a door. "Ohoooo!" cried the Captain. "You are magnificent here. Monte-Cristo, on my word of honor." The Mayor, a man of substance who owned the quarry, had a sitting room full of stuffed furniture. The Captain pointed to a yellowish framed photograph of a heavily-bearded man. "Father Christmas?" he said. "Or Karl Mordecai Marx?"

"My father, Captain. A good man."

"That is not a man: it is a forest. . . . Register of villagers, please. Move fast!"

The Captain glanced at the list, meticulously written in glossy black ink. "Uh-um! Three students here, I perceive. Oh, learned village of Dudicka! Hm. . . ."

The Mayor said: "Karel Benedikt will have died by this morning. He was dying of pneumonia yesterday morning: he cannot have lasted the night."

"What a misfortune, my dear sir, what a terrible thing. Who is Marek, Max . . . Medical Student?"

"Max Marek?" He's going to be a doctor: a decent boy."

"You make everything beautifully clear. If you hadn't told me I should never have known that a medical student intended to become a doctor. Thanks, best thanks."

Hoza bit his mustache, but managed to say: "Welcome."

"Skalda, Karel?"

"Karel Skalda is studying to be a lawyer, or was. He is not here: he is conscripted for heavy labor, Captain."

"Any strangers?"

"None."

"None, *Captain*."

"None, Captain."

"Have you any coffee?"

"A sort of coffee, Captain."

"Tell your wife to make some."

Hoza bellowed: "Etta! Coffee!"

"How old is your daughter?"

"Thirty, Captain."

"A widow, a merry widow." The Captain whistled a tune. "Now . . ." He paused, and asked with heavy irony whether he might smoke; said: "You are too, too kind," and lit a cigarette. There was a second of silence.

Then, quite distinctly, they heard a roar in the near distance.

It was a roar of laughter.

"Who can be laughing?" asked Mr. Hoza, filling his pipe.

The Captain said: "I rather doubt whether it will be any friends of yours. . . . Mayor Hoza!"

"Captain?"

"Did I give you permission to smoke?"

"I——"

Mrs. Hoza had come in with the coffee. She said: "They are laughing in the Kobras' place, I think."

"Now I wonder what they've found to laugh at?" said the Captain, looking at his watch. The Hozas looked at each other.

* * * * *

The Kobra house was only fifty yards away. Three men were laughing there.

A Corporal Hardtmuth had seen a man slinking by a wall in the vague light of the dawn, and had followed him. The man had peered into a window, and tapped at a door. The door had opened and the man had disappeared. Hardtmuth peeped through the window. Two more soldiers came on tiptoe. He waved them to silence, beckoned to them. They all peeped. Hardtmuth winked, grinning with delight, and laid his hand on the latch on the door. "Now," he whispered, and burst in with a savage growl thrusting his sub-machine-gun in front of him. "Stop!" he said. "Don't move. Don't move an inch. Don't bat an eyelid or I'll rip your guts out!"

A soldier said: "She's just in the right position for that, Corporal."

Hardtmuth advanced. "You get up," he said. "No —you lie perfectly still, ma'am. *You* get up. That's it. No, don't bother about your trousers. Keep still or I fire. Keep your hands up over your head. Right up. That's right. . . . And you on the bed there— keep still, I said. Still, I say! Who told you to move that leg? Keep them just where they are, *exactly* where they are. . . . Gentlemen, a penny to see the show!"

They walked around, staring, grasping their Schmeissers, laughing. The woman began to weep. She lay spread-eagled, sobbing. Large tears ran over her red cheeks.

"These redheads," said the Corporal. "Boy, is she red?"

"Warm material, that," said one of the soldiers; and the other added: "Belly looks as if it'd burst into flames."

"A real incendiary bomb," said Hardtmuth. "No, don't move lady, or so help me God I'll——"

"Please, sir, let me get up."

"Lie still!"

"Please let me cover myself up."

"What's your hurry? You weren't in such a hurry to cover yourself up two minutes ago, were you, Red?"

Footsteps sounded outside. She whispered, gasping with terror: "That's Jaromir! He's come back!"

Corporal Hardtmuth pressed the muzzle of his gun into her side and said: "Lie still!" He looked at her bosom, which heaved like a sea, and at her white skin and fiery hair. "Ginger," he said. The door opened. A big-boned dark man came in, treading heavily with thick-soled old boots. One of the soldiers met him and pushed a gun-muzzle into his stomach.

"Your old lady, I believe?" said the Corporal, giggling.

"What?" said the man, staring.

"We didn't do anything," said the soldier by the bed. "She was like this when we came in, wasn't she, Corporal?"

"God's truth," said Corporal Hardtmuth. "Exactly like this. Only we peeled that one off. Know him? We haven't had time to dress him again."

"Svatek!" said the big-boned man.

"The woman sobbed: "Ladislav! . . . Ladislav!"

The man called Svatek, standing with his hands above his head, said: "Ladislav. I . . ."

"What *do* you say in a case like that?" asked the Corporal, genially. "What *is* there to say?"

"You were waiting till I went to the quarry," said Ladislav.

Svatek shrugged his shoulders, and hung his head.

It was then that the soldiers began to laugh. They shouted with laughter. Ladislav Kobra also bowed his head, while the woman wept. When the laughter had died a little, the Corporal said: "Look, friend. I'll do you a favor." He stood behind Svatek, holding his Schmeisser against his naked back. "Go on, Ladislav, hit him. Hit him hard. Go on, kick him— he's just in the right position for a nice kick. Kick him where it'll teach him a lesson. Make an example of what you kick. Teach 'em to stay away from your good lady. I mean it: I'm doing you a favor. Let him have it, Ladislav my lad. Give it to him good."

One of the soldiers suddenly scowled and said: "When you come to think of it . . . as soon as your back's turned . . . why, God damn it and blast it to hell! Men they want! Why——"

"Hit him," said the Corporal.

Ladislav Kobra walked very slowly over to where Svatek stood. Svatek's long, thin body was covered, suddenly, with drops of sweat. "Ladislav!" he said. "Ladislav! This isn't my fault! She begged me to. She worried me till I did. She made me do it. It isn't my fault!"

Ladislav spat in his face.

"Now kick him," said the Corporal. Ladislav drew back a great boot, studded with iron nails. He measured his distance. "Now," said the Corporal.

Ladislav's foot paused, then fell to the floor.

"He's lying," said the woman. "He begged me, begged and prayed."

"Kick!" shouted the Corporal.

"No," said Ladislav, with tears in his eyes. "No. I will not, because I have given you enough to amuse you for one morning." He said to Svatek: "Later on I will kill you." He stepped back, took off his cap and dropped it so that it covered his wife. The Corporal flicked it away and knocked him down with the barrel of his gun. "I'll teach you to disobey orders, Slav," he said. Then, turning to Svatek he said: "If he won't, I will."

"Wait," said Svatek. "Don't. I don't know what you're here for, but I can help you. I can help you. I swear I can help you. I know everybody here. I know everything here. I can help you. Don't hit me."

The Corporal smacked him in the face and kicked him on the knee. "Dress," he said, "and come with me. You come, too, you men. You, Ginger, stay here: if you leave the house you will be shot. You stay too, Ladislav, my dear heart's friend, and argue it out with fire-belly over there."

The soldiers left, driving Svatek before them. Ladislav sat up on the floor and looked at his wife. He said nothing. She said nothing, but arose and ran into the kitchen, slamming the door. A minute later Ladislav followed her. She was kneeling on the floor, with her head hanging over a chair: she had cut her throat with a meat knife.

Out in the road, Svatek grinned and wiped Ladislav's saliva from his face. "We are all men of the world," he said. And he was no more than a hundred yards away when Ladislav, tearing his hair, began to howl like a dog.

The soldier who had scowled was cursing under his breath. The other soldier said to the Corporal: "His wife is a redhead."

The Mareks, on the outskirts of the village, heard Ladislav crying out. It was a nightmarish sound. For a moment their hearts seemed to shrink.

"I said, Doom," said Karel Marek.

V

Marek Launches a Boat

KAREL MAREK was a strong and candid soul, a wise and simple man who, in sixty years, had never entirely lost the limpid and dreamy peace of spirit that comes to happy children in the summer time. This made him beautful: a fall from a horse had damaged his nose, but iron hoofs could not have stamped out of his face the gentle radiance that illuminated it. An old woman had likened him to a good stove, that takes any bit of rubbish and turns it into grateful warmth, kindly fire.

Malleable elements, well-balanced, blend to form imperishable bronze. So it was with Karel Marek: age had not rusted him; time had given him graciousness and power. You felt that if something smashed Karel Marek until nothing but a fragment of him remained, a stranger might pick up that fragment and recognize it as part of a masterpiece. He was designed to teach as a pen is designed to write, or as a plowshare is designed to open soil to seeds and the rain. If he had been born in the dawn of things, if there had been no history, no geography, no reading, writing, or reckoning, Marek would still have been a teacher: children would have followed him as birds follow a hopeful wind, and he would have instructed them in the meaning of courage, courtesy and honor, and told them how these things were necessary, like skill in toil, to the soul of man that must go upwards out of the dirt.

*　　*　　*　　*　　*

Karel Marek laid his right hand on Max's shoulder, and took Anna by the arm. His face had not changed; but the touch of his hands had. He pinched. His long square fingers hurt Anna's arm, and even Max, a thick-shouldered man wearing a thick coat, was uncomfortably aware of a steely pressure near his collar bone. They both looked at Marek. His eyes were cold and deep, steady as wells of water. Marek began to talk. They felt a sensation of shock. The old caressing voice had become brittle. It cracked and broke like glass, snapping off sharp-edged words.

He said: "I want you to obey me without question," and pulled them into the house; dragged out a large ring on which three keys tinkled, opened a

[53]

drawer, pulled out a little packet of money and
thrust it into Max's pocket. "You are like my own
children, brother and sister. Anna, you must help
him: Max, you must help her. You must take each
other away, anywhere. Go through the woods and
get away, get out, get out of the parish, trust God
and try and get out of the country, anywhere. Do
you hear me? Anywhere away from Dudicka.
Quickly. You must do as I say."

Max said: "Why?"

Marek replied: "You heard that von Bertsch was
shot. You heard they were offering a huge reward.
You saw what came down. Men on parachutes: you
saw. You heard those shots. You heard that yell. It
was a man, not a dog in pain, a man in pain. Take
this money . . ." He ran into another room and returned, in five seconds, with a lump of meat, a piece
of bread, and an onion; pushed them into Max's
hand. "They have come here for blood. Dudicka will
pay for Bertsch. You are young, you must go. There
is a chance. God is good. You are innocent. You
must survive. Have no fear, but go, quick. Nobody
will touch me, everybody knows I am old, harmless.
Do as I say. Don't say a word. Get out, get out
fast."

"What are you asking us to do?" said Max.

"Max," said Marek. "Anna. I have never ordered
you to do anything. I have never begged you to do

anything for me. I'm begging you now. I am order-
ing you now. Take this, and go at once, anywhere,
out of Dudicka, out of the parish, as far away as you
can go. Lose yourselves, hide yourselves. Later on it
will be all right. You must do what I tell you. You
have got to do it. There is danger here—for you, not
for me."

"Why not for you?" asked Max.

"Because everybody knows me. Everybody knows
I have not been out of Dudicka in almost a generation. You are a student, a student is a danger. Anna
is a girl, she is a victim. Go away, now, and later
you will come back. Hide for a while and then go on.
Max, do you remember the woods? You used to
know the woods."

"I remember the woods," said Max.

"Go there. Wait a day. If need be, two, three
days. Then go on. Have I ever lied to you?"

They both said: "No, never."

"I swear to you that I shall be safe. Perhaps it is
all a mistake and I am mad. Only do as I say: now.
Don't wait to pack anything. Go. Goodby."

"But——"

For the first and last time in recorded history the
schoolmaster Karel Marek laid violent hands upon a
fellow human being. He seized Max by the collar
and the elbow and ran him out of the house. Then he
·paused for an instant and tears came into his eyes as

he said: "You are her brother and she is your sister."

Max replied, softly: "That was yesterday. Soon, I shall be her husband and she will be my wife."

For half a second amazement froze Marek's face. Then light broke through it like a sun through an overcast sky. He said: "Then go all the quicker. We'll meet soon. God be with you."

They hardly said goodby. A tone of fierce command in the voice of Karel Marek had something terrifying about it; something unarguable. They began to run into the woods. Karel Marek said: "I wish I had known this before," and blinked. The bottom of his garden touched the stream: there was a little bridge that he had built. Max and Anna crossed this bridge—it was only six feet long—and then the mâquis seemed to swallow and digest them. Karel Marek turned on his heel and went back into the house. Everything was quiet again. Max's hat was lying on a chair, a very old felt hat of a greenish tint gone yellow like a leaf about to die. Marek stroked it. Then he sat down at his table, half-instinctively picked up a pen and dipped it in ink. He laughed very softly: on this morning of all the mornings in his life he felt that his head was full of fine stories and clear-cut sentences. He listened. If anything was stirring he could not hear it. A tremendous peace seemed to have fallen upon the earth.

Marek wrote:—

The Bird That Wanted To Go Back To The Mud.

He added: *A Fairy Story By Karel Marek.*

Then, in his round clear handwriting, he wrote the following:—

"Once upon a time, millions and millions of years ago, when all the world was mud and slime and there was nothing living but long and slippery reptiles in the mud and insects in the air, a certain mud-lizard looked up out of a swamp and saw a flying bug. He leaped up to eat it but the bug flew always a little out of his reach, and so the mud-lizard kept leaping and leaping, flapping his claws in a strenuous effort to reach the bright flying bug that his heart desired. Hopeless! Or so it seemed; because the lizard belonged to the mud, and the bug belonged to the air. Well, children, for fifty thousand million years the mud-lizard leaped up, flapping his claws . . . and gradually a miracle happened. He tried so hard, you see. The muscles of his shoulders grew stronger, and his straining forelegs grew longer, and the end of it was that this mud-lizard one day struggled up after the bug, waved his claws, and rose into the air! His legs had become wings. He had, by unending toil and perseverance, left the slime for a finer and rarer element—he had become a bird!

[57]

And, full of joy, he flapped his wings and soared higher and higher. In vain, now, did the little bright bug try to escape him. The bird that had been a lizard pursued him and devoured him, and lived for a long time flying in the air and chasing bright insects; and all the time his wings got stronger and better so that, upon my soul, I really believe he could have flown up to the sun if he had put his mind to it! But one day while the new-born bird was flying over a great, deep, dirty and horrible marsh of mud and slime, he looked down and saw, swimming in the depths of the filthy water, a fat white grub. 'Oh,' sighed the lizard-bird, 'what would I not give for that lovely, juicy grub!' And thereupon, overcome with a desire for it, he plunged down into the marsh. Gone, alas, was the memory of his millions of years of struggle and strife and pain to get out of the mud into the sunlight! He plunged, I say. And being, now, no longer a thing of the mud and slime, but a winged creature of the air, he sank: the mud clung to him and he was drowned in it, and so he went back through his own foolishness to the place where he had begun."

He drew a charming little curly line terminating in a loop; then added, in little writing: "Max and Anna, my children, I do not think that we shall ever meet again. I have told you many little stories when you were children and I was younger; but this is the last story I shall have time to tell. Yet, I hope and believe that by God's grace there will come after me a teacher who will tell another story. My blessing. Uncle Karel."

Holding the sheet of paper, he went out into the garden again. Out of the back of his mind crept a memory of something he had read. He began to fold the sheet of paper, smiling meanwhile . . . a strange little one-sided smile that was almost apologetic. In the distance he could hear heavy footsteps. He found that he was standing by the bridge, under which ran a tiny tributary of the little Dudicka Stream.

He was aware, also, of unseen eyes watching him.

He called, very quietly: "Duda!"

A queer, hushed voice said: "Teacher?" A piece of woodland seemed to detach itself from the countryside. Something brownish emerged, with a rustle of leaves. It was a man, or something in the shape of a man. He was thin and supple, with matted hair and a tangled beard: he might have looked fierce, but for the wandering vacancy of his staring blue eyes. He was dressed in a coat and trousers frayed out to indescribable rags. About his neck was wound a bit of pink cotton. He had hung himself with leaves, flowers, and bits of metal and glass. His hands were narrow, hairy, and nailed like a dog's paws; his teeth shone white.

"Duda," said Marek, "come here."

The thing that looked like a man came crouching, almost on all fours. He looked at the paper in Marek's hands; raised his eyebrows, smiled an empty smile and said:

"Teacher . . . boats . . ."

The footsteps were coming nearer. "Yes, Duda, boats." Karel Marek bent the folded paper into a little boat and gave it to Duda, who, chuckling, placed it on the surface of the water. Tiny waves, scarcely bigger than thimbles, picked the paper boat up and drove it away. It sailed. Duda clapped his hands.

Karel Marek took out his watch, dragged the chain out of its buttonhole, and held it up. Duda laughed. Marek said: "Duda. Max and Anna, Duda —Max and Anna. In the forest. Look . . ." He gave Duda the watch and chain. "For you. Now you must do something for me. Max and Anna: they must hide. Help them. Go now."

He glanced towards the road. It was a rapid glance, and it caught a flash of light on a helmet. By the time he had looked back again, Duda had gone. He had shot into the bushes like a snake. Karel Marek whose ears were attuned to every whisper of the countryside had not heard him.

[60]

A boot kicked a wooden gate. Feet stamped. A big soldier in the uniform of a parachute jumper came running up followed by two more. He pushed the muzzle of a Schmeisser sub-machine-gun into Marek's lean belly and said:

"If you resist you will be shot."

Marek smiled. "And if I do not resist?" he said.

He turned his back and walked, very slowly, to the door of his house. Marek did not want the Germans to see his eyes, because he could not stop himself looking towards the forest.

It was quiet; slightly stirring, like a drop-scene in a romantic comedy.

"Who lives with you here?" asked the foremost soldier.

"Nobody," said Marek. They were already inside the house. The Germans looked about them. One of them went to Marek's desk. Another went from room to room: they heard his voice crying *Anybody here?* through each doorway. The man at the desk poked at a mess of papers. He carried his Schmeisser under his right arm.

"What are these?" he asked.

"Papers."

"Fritsch, you know Czech—what's this stuff?"

The soldier called Fritsch came lounging over. He looked at a sheet of notepaper: read aloud, stiffly, in fairly good Czech:—

[61]

"SALVAGE." He added: "It is in rhyme:—

> "I scooped up the scattered stars
> Dropped like nuts from passing cars;
> Chiseled off the iron heel
> Of the crescent moon, for steel.
> As the dawn began to blink
> I broke up its light for zinc.
> Heavy was my day, and dead,
> So I tore it down, for lead.
> Then I saw Apollo pass;
> Shore his shining hair, for brass;
> Cracked candescent suns for bent
> Bits of tungsten filament.
> See my bruised and bleeding back
> And my swollen salvage-sack!
>
> All is saved. So now you may
> Sing to drive the dark away."

"What's that in proper language?"

Fritsch frowned, and said: "It means something like this:—

Vehicles passing by scattered certain heavenly bodies like nuts . . . you know, bolts, screws, and so on. *For steel I chiseled off the iron heel of the crescent moon. It was at dawn. I smashed its light and got zinc. My day of death was heavy: I took lead from it. A brazen-haired man called Appollon passed. He had recently had a haircut. Fiery suns were destroyed for wires. My back is bruised and bleeding but my bag is swollen. We shall be saved. You may now sing to chase away the dark.* At the end, some initials, *K.M.*"

"I don't like the sound of that," said the first soldier. "Do you get that *Chase away the dark* stuff?"

"*Passing vehicles,*" said Fritsch.

"*Crescent moon*—hey, do you realize——?"

Marek said, in German: "What is all the fuss about? It is a little bit of poor verse."

"A poet, eh?" said Fritsch. "You don't know what happened at the New Moon, do you?"

"I wrote that weeks ago," said Marek. "When your people were collecting scrap metal again. You were taking lamps and things. It was meant to be nothing more than mild irony."

Then the third soldier came back, grinning, waving a nightdress. "He's lying," he said. "There's a woman here. Look at this. Feel it. It's still warm. Take a sniff at it, Fritsch—go on!"

"Um-um!" said Fritsch. "A man of his age."

"Dirty-mouth," said Marek; and Fritsch slapped his face.

"Three beds have been slept in," said the soldier with the nightdress. "Where are the other two people?"

[63]

"My nephew and adopted daughter," said Marek, calmly. "They left early this morning."

"For where?"

"They left."

"When?"

"Early."

"Where did they go?"

"Out."

The man with the nightdress sniffed it again and dropped it reluctantly. "Do you want half a pound of lead in your belly?" he asked, raising his gun.

"That would at least be *something* in one's belly," said Marek.

Fritsch pocketed the paper and said: "I'm taking him down. One of you had better stay here."

He drove Marek before him. The village street was full of people. As they approached the Mayor's house, Marek saw the priest limping along while a soldier grasped his collar.

The priest nodded, breathless. Karel Marek smiled and said: "Congratulate me, Father—I have at last written a poem which has caused a minor sensation."

"And I have just witnessed another Calvary," said the priest.

VI

The Other Side of Christ

W~HAT HAD HAPPENED~ was this:—

A soldier, a thickset Bavarian, drunk with the
rushing air and high-strung tension of his descent,
had reached the door of the little church. He pushed
it, and it opened. Inside, the church was dark and
silent. He crept in. The darkness blinded him. He
shouted: "Everybody keep still!" There was no answer. He became aware of a disquieting, sweetish
scent . . . a smell of something pleasant gone stale,
mixed with dust and a lingering memory of perspira-
tion. His eyes adjusting themselves to the gloom
picked out benches. He walked in on tiptoe, shouted
again. He was uneasy. He felt that somebody was
watching him. He would have sworn that eyes were
staring at him, that a man, or something, was standing close behind him. In a passage somewhere near
where he stood, he could hear quiet footsteps. Hold-

ing his Schmeisser gun, he swung round, covered a dark doorway and said: "Come out of there. I can see you. If you resist you will be shot." And then it seemed to him that the eyes were still watching him. Something cold crawled up his back, or so he imagined. He spun round on his heel. A white figure was standing not more than three yards away from him. It was tall and thin, and its hands were raised above its head. Instinctively, the soldier fired a burst of five shots. The figure did not move.

Then another door opened, and light came streaming in. The soldier turned to face it. The priest stood, blackly silhouetted against an oblong of dawn, saying: "What is this?"

"Hands up."

The priest raised his hands. He was an old man, somewhat rheumatic. He could not raise his hands straight above his head. He walked towards the soldier. The soldier saw a strange, stricken look in the old man's eyes, and followed it. He turned his head. The priest was looking at the white figure that had frightened him in the dark. It was the figure of a great wooden Christ, hanging upon a black wooden cross. The head of Christ hung down on his left shoulder. The artist had carved the shape of blood-drops running down from the crown of thorns, the nail-wounds in hands and feet, and the spear-wound in the left side.

[66]

In the right side of Christ a new wound had appeared: a perfect cluster of five bulletholes.

The priest said: "What have you done?"

For perhaps the tenth part of a second the soldier hesitated. For that space of time he experienced a pang of fear. He remembered, in a flash, something ancient and awful . . . a flash, a dream-flash, of blue smoke, solemn yellow candle flames, and white cloth swaying, and the great vibrant drone of an organ. Then it was gone. He caught the priest by his collar. The old man was wearing a greasy old dressing-gown and a pair of trousers. The soldier dragged him out into the street and pushed him forward at arm's length.

It was then that Marek spoke to the priest, and the priest replied:

"I have just witnessed another Calvary."

To this, Karel Marek replied in a voice strangely exalted:

"This morning every hill is a Calvary and every garden is Gethsemane."

Then, for an instant, everybody paused, because above all the other noises that had broken out in Dudicka there rose one noise that sounded . . . how is one to describe that noise? Can you imagine a mourning of enchanted bells? An agony of melancholy gongs? . . . It was something unmistakably inhuman; and yet it resembled nothing in heaven or on earth so closely as it resembled human grief. It sobbed, shivered, and died away.

Then there was a noise like water boiling: this came from people's lips.

Simultaneously, everybody said: *"Balaban!"*

* * * * *

The glass-maker, Jan Balaban, had one great grief. The Balaban Tear-glass would die with him. He, and his ancestors, had made the thin and beautiful goblets that sighed, trembled, and rang with a strange and poignant sound like a sob. He, too, had made them. Now, his lungs were finished, and his sons could not make glass weep. It was Jan Balaban who had said: "It is in our breath." His three sons, Ludvik, Alois, and Jakub, were fine workmen. Yet, it seemed, they lacked that thing which came from God. The time had been when the old man had flown into terrible rages, cursing his wife whom he blamed for having, somehow, somewhere in her body and blood, sucked in and drained away the glory that was in the Balaban breath. He had cursed his sons, too, calling them fat oxen like their mother and telling them that they were meat, dead red meat. It is true that they were all big redfaced men. When the disappointment of it rose up into his throat he would cry and wash it down again with brandy; drink at the inn until he was exceedingly drunk . . . strike the innkeeper's clumsy cheap glasses with his fingers; listen, burst into tears, and say: "If you cannot weep, let me weep for you." At this point the innkeeper judiciously removed every glass within reach of Balaban. He knew the old man. In him, tears preceded a great rumble and flash of anger, just as heavy raindrops precede thunder and lightning. Ludvik, Alois and Jakub worshiped him with a kind of dumb, wounded adoration. They were ponderous and silent as he was wizened and voluble. "Swedes," he would say. "You are Swedes. You should go to Sweden and make chamberpots an inch thick with little sailing boats on them, or vases shaped like spittoons with *A Present For a Good Girl* around the edges. Go, go to Sweden, go to hell!" And they would say: "Yes."

Then old Jan Balaban begged their pardon and opened the great oak cupboard. This cupboard contained his yesterdays. Upon its shelves stood about twenty glasses of various shapes, some of the finest examples of the work of the Balabans. The oldest of them had been made by a Balaban in 1693. The newest was the work of Jan himself in 1898; it was as good as any. The largest of them all was a fantastic piece—an oval bowl three feet long and two feet deep, of an almost imperceptible pale blue, "the color of air," but of great thickness and weight. It was nevertheless flawless, "My sons, like a summer

sky," and perfectly translucent. It had been made in
1770, at the request of some lunatic nobleman who
had died before it was completed. He had had some
notion of filling it with wine, for God knows what
bizarre and improper purpose. Only wine had killed
him first and the bowl stayed with the Balabans,
monumental and useless as the Pyramids. In the
bottom of the bowl there was inlaid a gold medallion
almost as large as a coffee saucer, engraved with the
portrait of the nobleman, and his motto *Quid Si
Cœlam Ruat?* This fabulous vessel was known as
the Balaban Bowl, and, in resonance, it was the
Balaban masterpiece. It had an unbelievable sen-
sitivity. If you sang into it it picked up the vibra-
tions of your voice and, transmuting them into something of a golden melancholy, hurled them back at
you in stunning volume. If you touched it, ever so
lightly with a finger, it sighed and sobbed for ten
minutes by the clock.

Old Balaban would show them all these things,
ring the glasses and goblets one by one and cry:
"Must this go? Must this perish? God breathed into
clay and made clay man! The Balabans breathe into
sand and make sand sing! Who else will do this if
you do not: I am old, my breath is gone, but listen
. . ." And he always drew a wet finger round the edge
of the Balaban Bowl, which first purred and then

wept and then, with a sobbing sigh became silent.
Then Jan became silent too.

*   *   *   *   *

He came down that dawn to find his silent sons
standing stolidly near the furnace, while a Sergeant
and two soldiers stood with Schmeissers in the doorway. He said:

"What is it?"

The Sergeant said: "If you resist you will be
shot."

"Resist what?"

"Who lives here?"

Jan replied: "Me and my three sons. We are the
Balabans."

The Sergeant was well known as a joker. It was
said that he could make you die laughing. His name
was Bauer. He said: "So?" His voice was low, tremulous, full of awe. "You are the Balabans?"

"You have heard of us I see?" said the old man.

Sergeant Bauer bowed low until the muzzle of his
gun touched the floor. Jan blinked at him with his
inflamed eyes, and then smiled and said: "But what
brings you here?"

Sergeant Bauer said: "Why, Herr Caravan——"

"Pardon, *Balaban*."

"Forgive me, Herr Latheran——"

"Excuse me, sir, *Balaban*."

[71]

The Sergeant laughed and said: "For the moment, upon my word, I thought you said Balaban. Well, sir, we have been sent personally to visit you by no less a person than the Fuehrer, Adolf Hitler. And what do you think of that?"

It was only then that old Jan began to see that the Sergeant was laughing at him, but he said: "The Emperor Franz Josef bought glasses from me. Why not the Fuehrer?"

The Sergeant grinned. "Why not?" he said.

Jan Balaban said: "Unhappily, there is no more tear-glass, but——"

"What a pity, no more tear-glass," said Sergeant Bauer. "I did so want a tear-glass!"

Then Jan Balaban took out a key and opened his cupboard. On the shelves the glasses glinted, while on the floor the Balaban Bowl picked up half the dawn. Then he seemed to recover himself; shut the cupboard and locked it. The Sergeant strode over, neatly picked the key from between Balaban's fingers and opened the cupboard again. He looked down at the great bowl. He said: "I could use a glass like that for beer," and spat into the bowl. The bowl sobbed. "Hey!" said the Sergeant, "did you hear that? Listen!" He spat again. The bowl, still vibrating, sobbed louder.

Jan tried to stop him, but Bauer held him off with one hand. The three sons moved like one: two

Schmeissers jerked up at them, and they stood still. "What's that on the bottom?" asked Sergeant Bauer.

"That," said Balaban, "is a gold medallion of the Baron——"

"—The *what* madallion?"

"The gold medallion of the——"

"Oh-oh," said Sergeant Bauer. What he did then was unimaginable. He gave his gun to a soldier to hold, stooped, grabbed the bowl, heaved with a grunt, and held it above his head: he was a man of great strength. All the Balabans cried out together. They did not dare to move. Bauer opened his hands, and the Balaban Bowl fell onto the brick floor. The terrible clangor and the atrocious sobbing of its destruction was what all Dudicka heard. And then everybody said *"Balaban!"*

The old man stood, paralyzed. His three big sons rushed forward. The soldiers fell back. Bauer roared: "Not one more move!" Ludvik, Alois and Jakub stopped: the Schmeissers were leveled. They looked at the old man. He was standing perfectly still; not even his red eyes, which always blinked, were moving. Bauer stooped and picked up the medallion, weighed it in his hand, whistled with something like awe, and dropped it into a pocket. It dragged his clothes down into a grotesque sag on that side. Then he said: "You two stay here and don't let these bastards move!"

He went to the door, paused, came back and said: "I've never heard anything like that in my life"; picked up the goblet of 1693, rang it, and dropped it. There was nothing of it left but some curved fragments and a floating sob . . . then nothing but the fragments. With the barrel of his gun Sergeant Bauer swept the shelves. You might have thought that the historic glasses of Balaban were weeping over the smashed remains of the Balaban Bowl. "Good!" said Sergeant Bauer, and went out.

One glass was left unbroken. It was a little cup that Jan's father had made. Moving like a puppet with stiff joints, old Jan picked it up and, staring straight in front of him, clasped it to his bosom under his shirt. Then he said, in a thin voice: "And so it all comes down to little bits of glass for Duda to play with."

VII

Those Whom the Gods Would Cast Away

You may keep a dozen generations of weaver birds caged, in captivity. Then, if you set free a bird of the thirteenth generation, it will fly away and weave itself a nest of infinite intricacy. Thus, the man called Duda, offspring of a quarryman's widow and an unknown father, had taken to the woods. His name was Hugo, but he had never been able to pronounce it. As a child he called himself *Duda*. Not even Karel Marek had been able to teach him the things that people, in this century, need to know. To Duda, figures and letters were mysteries, a printed page was a gray blur and a story said nothing. He could not hook together twenty words. He was jumpy, incalculable, and shy of human company. Even pictures told him nothing. He liked colors for their own sake. He would steal, like a jackdaw, anything bright enough to attract his eye.

The patience and forbearance of ten Mareks could not have inspired him with a sense of right and wrong: this was, simply, something he was not made to contain. He was regarded as an idiot: nearly every village has its idiot. By the time he was eight years old he had slipped away into the woods. He was harder to hold than a puff of smoke; quick and light as a gnat. No corner of the forest was unknown to him: it was said that he knew where every leaf was, and would know if somebody moved a twig. There was something inhuman in his agility; no man ever climbed as he climbed or ran as he ran. Nobody knew where he slept, or, indeed, if he slept—nobody had ever seen him asleep. He liked animals. People had learned to take care how they did Duda a favor: he had his own conception of a desirable gift. Once, Mrs. Kafka gave him some colored beads. The next morning she found that he had brought her six young hedgehogs. Karel Marek, who always had a sympathy with creatures forgotten of God, used to save tinfoil off tobacco packets and odds and ends of metal and glass, which he used to leave at the bottom of the garden. Duda would creep out in the dead of night to collect them. It was impossible to see him if he did not want to be seen, and when he did show himself it was with a certain shy reluctance. It was believed that he hoarded nuts and roots, like an animal, to feed him in the winter. But sometimes, if a winter were extraordinarily severe, Duda would come into the village. In thirty degrees of frost he could walk, dressed only in trousers, jacket, and odd rags, into the teeth of a raging wind. He never felt cold; he was impervious to everything except hunger. He would come into the village stepping gingerly, watching everything and everybody, ready to disappear in a bound. People gave him food. He always took it away to eat it, always ate alone. His pockets were never empty: he carried little animals about with him—squirrels, rabbits, mice, young birds. If ever you found one of these, running or flying in your house or lying in a little nest on your doorstep you knew that you had somehow earned Duda's approval. He did not tame animals; they simply acknowledged him as one of themselves. He lived by memories behind the mind; could sniff things out like a dog, see in the dark like a cat, run for hours without tiring in a long and wolfish lope. His mother had run away from him, terrified as of a judgment of heaven. He lived alone in a world of green shadows, crowing over his hidden treasures of shiny junk.

For Marek, he had an almost instinctive devotion: he remembered the gentle old man as a dog remembers a master . . . the trees had called him away, but he had to come back sometimes if only to look, or to bring a flower, or a dormouse, or an iridescent

beetle. He understood what Marek said to him. The
schoolmaster maintained that Duda possessed intelligence—intelligence of a strange kind, but intelligence . . . one simply had to speak Duda's language, employing, instead of ratiocination, sweet
things to eat and bright things to look at. "Are ordinary men so *very* different, bless them?" Marek
asked.

Duda slid through the woods, now, like a weasel.
Max and Anna believed that they were moving fast
and silently; but Duda could hear them crashing
through. Branches creaked and swung swishing back
. . . dead leaves rustled and dead twigs snapped . . .
little startled animals ran away and birds rose, terrified. Max and Anna had passed many of their hours
of play in those woods when they were children;
they could move more quietly than most people, but
Duda belonged to the woods. He did not need to see
them. He followed their sound. Also, he could smell
them. He kept a hundred yards behind them, darting
from tree to tree.

Soon, he heard them talking. He knew their voices,
but now their voices sounded different. It was not
merely that they were talking in whispers: their
whispering had a different quality. He had heard
them whispering before. Something made them
sound different . . . the kind of thing that changed
the voices of birds and beasts, and even the hum of

[78]

insects, at certain times of the year. If people built nests, then Max and Anna might be about to build a nest. *Hide*, Marek had said; *they* must hide . . . and floated a boat; and gave him the bright watch that ticked like a little heart . . . the shining thing that was cold but alive . . . hide . . . to make a nest?

Max was saying: "Beloved, it seems to me that we are not doing right in going away."

She replied: "He says so. Max, did you see his face? Let us do what he said."

"I'm afraid."

"For him?"

"For him and for you, Anna."

"Somehow," said Anna, "I am not afraid. I don't know why, but I am not afraid. I am not afraid, although I know that something is happening."

"Can somebody from Dudicka have killed Bertsch?" asked Max.

"I don't think so. They will make inquiries and then they will go away. Then we can go back."

Max looked at her and said: "It will not be so simple as that. They are not the kind of people to let it be as simple as that . . . Anna, did you see how his face lit up?"

"I wish we could have told him before. I wish it had happened before."

"I believe that things happen at their right time," said Max.

[79]

"No," said Anna. "Because I could have loved you all those years."

Max said: "I have heard what the Nazis have done in other villages. He has made us go away because he is afraid that we might be separated."

"But we have always been separated: he didn't know that it mattered. It didn't matter——"

"They have a way of cleaning villages out . . . the men to one place, the women to another place, and there is an end of everything. Perhaps he's heard something. Perhaps he knows something. He is such an old man, and such a good man, that there is no reason in the world why they should harm him. Is there?"

"No," said Anna. "I don't think I am afraid."

"I think I am a little bit afraid," said Max.

"Where shall we go?"

"I think that what we had better try to do is, get out of the wood on the east side, go across country to the road and try and get to Prague, Anna."

"I shall do whatever you say, anything you say."

Something dropped out of a tree. Max's hand covered Anna's mouth: she had opened it to scream. The thing that had fallen looked like a huge bundle of brush. It fell almost soundlessly and was a man. It was Duda. His face was contorted with fear. He stood in front of them, his arms outstretched. "No,"

[80]

he said. "No." He pointed over his shoulder with a skinny thumb. "No! Not! Not!"

"Duda," said Max. "What's the matter with you?" Duda held up Marek's watch, pointed to it, smiled, and said: "Hide." Max stretched out a hand and began to say, "That's Uncle Karel's watch——" but Duda had leaped back ten feet.

"For me," said Duda. "Max, Anna. Hide."

He grasped Max's sleeve and beckoned, leading them away to the left.

"I believe Uncle Karel has sent him," said Anna. "He would do anything for Uncle Karel."

"Uncle Karel," said Duda.

They followed him. He led them deeper and deeper into the forest, into the black heart of the forest.

"Where is he taking us?" whispered Anna.

Max replied: "I don't know, but one thing is certain—he knows these woods better than I know the palm of my hand, and I believe there is some story of caves . . ."

Duda stopped, and laid a finger against his lips. He looked at them in a kind of agonized appeal. They were silent. Duda stood still. They saw his nose quiver. He was smelling the air, leaning forward, intently listening. They heard nothing but the quiet busy whisper of the forest; but Duda could hear something more.

People were coming. They had a bad sound. He had no words to describe the sound of them: there are no words to describe it. There was too much metal about it . . . there was something heavy and dangerous in it. Big, hostile things were moving gently, trying to make no noise. He knew somehow that these were the things that had fallen out of the sky, and that these things had made a voice cry out in pain and that they were dangerous things. He darted forward, pausing occasionally to clench and unclench his hands in an agony of impatience while Max and Anna struggled after him. He could, by some miracle of suppleness, turn himself into a fluid and pour himself through impassable spaces. Max and Anna were struggling for breath, and drenched in sweat. They arrived, at last, at a rise in the ground. It was as if, in some forgotten age, the whole forest had sunk, leaving one flat, saucer-shaped hillock very densely covered with trees. Duda beckoned them into the shadows between these trees. Near the top of the little hill there stood a great old pine tree which had been struck by lightning. The flash had gouged out a splintery groove. Duda pointed to this. "It is a landmark," said Max. "He wants us to remember this place." Duda took them down beyond the hill, into a hideous and stony waste covered with a tangle of scrub. He stooped, peering from side to side, and grasped a great thorn-bush in his hard little hands. He heaved. The bush came away. It was Duda's door: it covered a hole in the ground. The hole went down, gently sloping, about three feet in diameter. It breathed out a smell of earth. "There," said Duda. They hesitated but he, agile as a fox, leaped down. Having shown them that it was safe he came up again. Max crept in; Anna, holding his hand, followed. Then Duda, grasping the bush, descended, sliding on his back and left the thorn-bush covering the entrance.

"Max, where are we?"

They stood in a heavy darkness full of the smell of dead leaves and musty soil. Max felt in his pocket, and found his lighter. He said: "Did I remember to put a flint in this machine?" It clicked and lit. In the light of its little blue flame they saw only an enormous blackness in front of them. Duda pulled them forward. "Wait," said Max, and fumbled again for his notebook. It was filled with notes of anatomy lectures, illustrated with diagrams drawn with infinite care in red, black, and yellow pencil. He tore out a page, touched it with the flame. It burned bright yellow. Duda was ten yards ahead of them, wildly beckoning. They crouched, but the hole in the ground was wider now. It was a cave, seven feet high. "Yes, yes, yes," said Duda. Anna, holding Max's hand, suddenly kissed it. The cave turned, left and right. The paper burned down. Max lit another page of his book. Suddenly, he laughed shortly and said: "Professor Synek promised me I would find these lectures illuminating." They both began to laugh, then, and Duda laughed too.

"How far does this cave go?" asked Max.

Duda said: "Deep, deep, deep, deep."

Three sheets of paper had burned away, when Anna said: "I think I see light." There was, indeed, a grayness in front of them. They turned again, to the right. Anna cried out: Max blinked. Before them lay something fantastic. Abruptly, the cave widened and became vast. From somewhere above them a faint light came down. It struggled through a crack in the earth, or rather, through a dozen cracks and crevices. The accumulated light that penetrated had, perhaps, the power of one bright candle; but it was reflected from a thousand twinkling points in the rock. Bits of quartz caught it and winked; the facets of innumerable prismatic crystals picked it up and sparkled. In one place a great mass of silica shimmered like a shovelful of yellow diamonds. The dark floor appeared to crawl with sparks like burned paper, and from the jagged incrustations overhead emerald and rose-colored lights hopped and darted like fireflies. "My God," said Max, and lit another sheet of paper. It was as if he had touched his flame to a huge set-piece in some stupendous fireworks display. The light seemed to explode. It rushed up, struck the roof, ricocheted off, cascaded from the walls and splashed from great bundles of hanging crystals which blazed like glass chandeliers at a banquet. All the colors in the world rushed together and broke up. The sparkling stuff underfoot swarmed with scurrying specks of flame. Then the paper went out. Blackness rushed in, and so, into this blackness, the dim diffusion of daylight seeped back.

"Is it real?" said Anna. "Are we awake? Are we asleep? Max, are there fairies? Where are we?"

Max said to Duda: "Where? Where, Duda?"

Duda waved his hand vaguely, and then pointed overhead. "Boom!" he said, throwing out his arms in a circle, and ducking his head. "Boom, boom!"

"I think," said Max, "I think he means the quarry. But it can't be."

"Could he mean the old slate quarry?" asked Anna.

"Perhaps we are somewhere near it. I don't know. I thought I knew these woods. . . . Duda, where are we? Quarry?"

Duda nodded.

"Which one?"

Duda shook his head and laughed. Then he beckoned them forward again. The cavern grew smaller. A kind of terror came into Duda's face. His eyes were luminous in the vague light. He pointed to the black mouth of another cave, shook his head, laid a

[85]

finger on his lips and said. "No." Max lit another
paper torch and looked into the darkness. He advanced a few paces. "No," said Duda.

"No what?" said Max.

Then, with hideous distinctness a dozen tremendous hollow voices shouted: *What? . . . What? . . .
What? . . . What? . . .* Anna clasped her hands to
her heart. "The echo," said Max. The voices replied: *"Oh . . . Oh . . . Oh . . . Oh. . . .* Max went
back to where Anna stood. The cave was cold. There
was a ghostliness in the twinkle of the lights. Duda,
at the other end of the domed cavern, was sitting
on his heels, looking at something. Max held the
last two inches of burning paper high above his head.
Duda was contemplating a mass of bits of metal,
colored cloth, and broken glass: he had arranged it
in a large crazy pattern. He placed Marek's watch
in the middle of it, upon a colored plate upon which
there was painted a picture of a blue dog. Next to
the watch he put a broken china cat with a yellow
coat and blue eyes: this was Duda's treasure-house.

Max and Anna looked at each other. He could see
her large eyes gleaming out of her white face. She
said:

"Max, what is he doing now?"

Quick as a monkey, Duda was plaiting twigs and
twisting branches into a crude oval. In the middle of

this he threw down soft branches of spruce. "It looks like a nest," said Max.

Duda smiled, pointed to them and then to the branches, and said: "Yes. Nest. You—a nest." And impulsively stooping again he snatched up something from his store of bright things and held it out in the palm of his hand. It was a glass marble decorated with a pink spiral.

Max said: "Good heavens, I remember that: I gave it to him when I was a little boy. He remembers."

Shivering with cold, Anna said: "What are we to do now?"

"We must wait and see what happens, but for the moment we are safe here."

VIII

The Brothers Svatek

MEANWHILE SVATEK—the man who had been caught with the redheaded woman—had gone into the presence of the Captain in the Mayor's house. Rudolf Svatek was the clown of Dudicka. He had a bright wit and a certain charm of manner. One never knew when he was serious or when he was not. He had a certain exaggeration of manner, an overemphasis of tone, that made serious matters sound light and light matters serious. People enjoyed his company: he had a reckless humor that made even death seem trivial when he talked about it. Of Rudolf Svatek the schoolmaster had said: "There is good in him; yes. But there is a glass of hundred-year-old brandy in a grape pip; only life is too short for a man to get it out." This was the one man on earth whom Marek personally disliked. That gentle and trusting soul distrusted Rudolf. He saw some-

thing sinister in his eternal jocularity. Rudolf was
the younger of two brothers. His elder brother,
Elias, was a plain man, laborious and slow as a
plow-horse, watchful of pennies, and prematurely
wrinkled by deep calculation. It was said that Elias
was the son of his father but that Rudolf was the
son of somebody who passed by. Elias, like his
father, was short and squat, with black eyes and
black hair, and a clipped black beard. But Rudolf
was tall and thin and had a queerly studious look;
nearsighted hazel eyes, long, prominent teeth, and a
wild head of dry brown hair thickly sprinkled with
gray. He had something of the destructiveness of a
malevolent pup; an irresponsible mischievousness
veined with malice. He had talked his way out of
many troubles. The people of Dudicka had never
met so glib a liar nor so shameless a man. He be-
wildered them. He begged with his right hand and
squandered with his left; left his wife and child
penniless while he treated casual acquaintances with
borrowed money; stole coins or garments behind a
screen of uproarious jokes; talked politics with
blood-curdling boldness, and at the same time slunk
in the shadow of a grin and a wink and a clownish
grimace. He was shiftless. His farm was a wilderness
out of which his wife tried to scratch enough to eat.
When she remonstrated with him (which was sel-
dom) he said that he was working things out: he

could crush her with terrifying silences and fits of sullenness which lasted for days. Occasionally he would disappear on some little unexplained adventure, and return, sometimes, with a little cash. In the presence of women he could be particularly captivating. They liked his dashing air of confidence and the way he made them laugh. He would tell his companions at the inn how, once, he had been to bed with a noblewoman; he had a certain flair for obscene description accompanied by graphic pantomime. Everybody said that he was good-natured, kind-hearted, sympathetic. Yet there were some who muttered that Rudolf listened patiently to your troubles in order to make comic conversation out of them for free brandy at the inn; and that his generosity was like that of the hunter who cut off his dog's tail and ate the meat and gave the bones to the dog. At forty he had the restlessness of a sixteen-year-old boy. He was one of those men of whom people ask: "Now why is he not a great success?" Elias said that Rudolf was simply lazy. A more cultivated observer might have seen in Rudolf something of the loose-lipped optimism of the bohemian-criminal type that trusts to luck, counts its chickens without having any eggs, and vaguely hopes to find a stray coin in every gutter.

By the time they had reached the Mayor's door, the Corporal and the soldiers had already begun to

think that Rudolf Svatek was not at all a bad kind
of fellow. He had wiped Ladislav's spit from his
face, grinned, held up his cuff, and made a comment
at once outrageously dirty and comical. Then, as if
he had known the Corporal for several years and
was bursting with the story, he began to tell him
about Ladislav's wife; what she had said to him,
what he had said to her, what she had told him
about Ladislav as a performer in the marriage-bed,
and how, crying "Rudolf! Rudolf!"—he imitated
her voice so ludicrously, and with so grotesque a
simulation of ecstasy that the Corporal burst out
laughing—she had performed all kinds of monstrous
tricks. Limping heavily, he congratulated the Corporal on the power of his kick and thanked heaven
that it was only his shin . . . laughed, bent his long
legs and walked like a man suffering with internal
injuries.

"Ah," he said, "all these people are mugs; God,
what mugs they are! It's nice to get acquainted with
some real people for a change . . . I mean people who
at least know how to make a quick move and aren't
scared of priests and all that rubbish. I can help
you guys. God Almighty, my principles are human-
itarian. Jesus, what the bloody hell do all these little
issues matter, really, when you consider everybody
and everything? For Christ's sake hurry up and
win the war. The sooner you win the better; then we

can settle down a bit, have a bit of quiet fun for a change . . . Look, don't make it too much of a broadcast, but you can pass the word to your officer that as it happens there's no secret in this village that I haven't stuck my nose into. What the men haven't told me the women have. If you get what I mean . . ." He grinned, uncovering his brown, prominent teeth. ". . . there's nothing *private* as far as I'm concerned. Rely on me."

The Corporal nodded. They went into Hoza's house. Many people were assembled there, now, mostly villagers guarded by soldiers with Schmeissers. Elias Svatek had been brought in and was standing against a wall, dark and thick as a treestump, scowling, his mouth compressed. Rudolf, in an almost inaudible whisper, said to the Corporal: "Remember, on the quiet."

But the Corporal stamped to attention, saluted stiffly, begged permission to speak, and snapped: "This man here, Rudolf Svatek, assures me that he has exact information concerning activities in this village!"

A murmur, something between a hiss and a groan, came from the Mayor and the villagers. Rudolf Svatek raised his eyebrows angrily, opened his mouth and said: "What, *me?*" He blinked and then, like a man indignant beyond endurance, shouted: "It's a slander and a lie. A lie and a slander! I never

[92]

said so! Hang me, shoot me, kill me—but even if I knew anything that you wanted to know I wouldn't tell you if you cut me to little pieces!"

At the same time he caught the Captain's eye, and his remarkably expressive face twitched itself, for a split second, into a grimace which said: *I'm only saying this for their benefit.*

The Captain walked slowly over and looked at Rudolf Svatek and said: "A diplomat, eh? A diplomat, by God! A Churchill, a Roosevelt, for God's sake! Now look, you. I know you. You want to run with the hare and hunt with the hounds, don't you? Don't you, eh? Eh?"

Rudolf shook his head. The Corporal, begging permission to speak, said: "He swore that he was familiar with everything and everybody in the village, sir. These men heard him. He asked permission to speak to you privately."

Rudolf Svatek turned his head. The eyes of every villager in the room were fixed on his. He made another quick grimace, an exquisite one with eyes, nose, forehead, and lips; and this grimace said: *It's all right, I'm just leading him up the garden.*

Elias Svatek, whose face had become almost black, suddenly found his voice and said: "Friends . . . friends . . ." He was strangling with shame and rage. His mouth made heavy clicking noises: like a man turning over a heap of cobblestones to find a

[93]

really heavy one to throw, Elias was rummaging in his heavy vocabulary for something terrible with which to express his agony. He said: "Friends . . . that thing is no Svatek! That thing is not my brother. That thing is not my father's son! If . . ." His face swelled and his voice came out in a rattling roar: "If that thing is my mother's son my mother was a whore!"

The Mayor said: "Be quiet, Elias. Don't say things you will be sorry for. Marta Svatek was a good woman . . . but any hen can lay an egg without a shell once in a while."

The priest said: "As bugs and fleas are necessary to warn us against dirt, so even such poor men are necessary in the scheme of the Almighty."

The Mayor's daughter, Etta Hertl, said: "But if one keeps oneself clean, is it just to have bugs and fleas?"

And the farmer, Roman Kafka, simply said: "The next time I see you I am going to kick your face in like a rotten walnut."

They all said these things together, against a background of astonished and indignant exclamations. Rudolf grinned; but there was rage in the twist of his mouth. He said to his brother: "What's the matter, Elias? Do you think I'm going to tell them where you've hidden your money?" The Captain was very silent: he was listening.

Elias said: "Neither you nor anybody else knows where I've hidden my money."

The Captain looked at him. Elias saw that exasperation had led him into something like a confession. But it was in the nature of the man to stand obstinately by anything he said, right or wrong. He said: "Yes, all right. I've got some money hidden away. Hidden, yes, hidden away. Find it. My father worked for it, I worked for it. Svatek works for Svatek. Not for anybody but Svatek, no, nobody. Try and find it! You'll have to take Dudicka to pieces bit by bit."

He said this to the Captain and turned his face away from Rudolf. The Captain said: "Why not?" Then he said to Rudolf: "Come into the other room with me."

Rudolf looked at the villagers there. Their eyes were like stones. He tried to make another grimace, but the muscles of his face were twitching. His expression had lost its eloquence and even its meaning. His face was only twisted. And everybody was staring at him. Then he said, suddenly, enraged, looking at the Mayor's daughter: "All the same— you wouldn't have minded having such bugs in your bed!"

The Corporal prodded him in the back with a Schmeisser. He followed the Captain out of the room. Etta Hertl said: "He is a liar. I never loved anybody but my husband, and when he died men stopped being men." Her mother put an arm over her shoulders and said: "When a rotten stick is burning it throws out sparks. Just brush them away."

Marek said: "It also sometimes crackles, Etta. At least, it hisses. But when did it ever tell the truth?"

The priest said: "God forgive me, I never did trust men that live on laughter. The strain makes them mad."

And Roman Kafka said: "When I get hold of him, Father, if he laughs you can call it a miracle."

*   *   *   *   *

Rudolf stood very straight. His face was grave. His mouth, closed as tight as he could close it, revealed only the ends of two brown front teeth. Then he smiled: it was a smile that was half-knowing and half-sheepish: women had fallen in love with his smile. The Captain said: "Open your mouth wider"; looked, and said: "Your teeth are rotten."

Rudolf replied, with charming ingratiation: "Ah . . . Sir . . . Captain . . . a decayed tooth is, as you might say, the poor man's savory."

"You are disgusting," said the Captain. "Now. Say what you have to say."

Rudolf said: "I know everything there is to know about the people here——"

"Say it then," said the Captain "And be quick,"

he added, with indescribable menace: "And truthful."

At this, Rudolf paused. The Captain, watching, saw a dampness appear on his cheeks and forehead, while tiny drops sprang up on his upper lip. Rudolf blinked, and, with an easy gesture, began to say: "Well, you see . . ."

In a voice like the ticking of a typewriter the Captain said: "Be concise, brief, and exact."

Rudolf said: "The schoolmaster, Karel Marek, is a pacifist and a revolutionary. You heard me say that Elias—that's my brother—has money hidden somewhere——"

"But he wouldn't give you any," said the Captain.

"It isn't that," said Rudolf.

"Devotion, no doubt, to the Third Reich?"

"Well . . . yes . . ."

"Then why didn't you report it before?"

"Well . . . you know how it is . . ."

"I don't know how it is; tell me how it is."

Rudolf sweated, and then, like a man inspired, he said: "He has guns concealed."

The Captain looked up. "What sort of guns?"

"I've seen at least one." Rudolf grinned. "He keeps it wrapped up in oily rags between a beam and the roof."

"When did you see this?"

"Well . . . yesterday morning."

"How? Why?"

"It . . . fell down by accident."

"However, you kept it to yourself."

"I . . . meant to mention it but it slipped out of my head. I've been in trouble . . . my wife has been ill, and, well . . . you know how it is . . ."

The easy charm of Rudolf Svatek which was so effective in a bar, where everything is accepted, now broke down. It crashed, became mere colored paper, like inflated currency. The Captain said: "Look here, my Slav friend, if you want to live, you understand, you will talk."

"Sir . . . sir . . . there is Roman Kafka. His son is a dangerous person."

"His son is now a labor conscript," said the Captain, calmly.

Rudolf was silent.

"And what about the Mayor?" asked the Captain.

"He hates the Germans," said Rudolf.

"You know that previously-elected mayors retain their office by special permission?" said the Captain.

Rudolf nodded.

"But you insinuate that we are incapable of selecting; you maintain that our chosen, or tolerated, heads of villages, are——"

"I . . ."

"Yes?"

"It is always possible for anybody, sir, to be mistaken once in a while."

"Specify, concerning the Mayor."

"He has expressed discontent, and even dislike, for . . . with . . . against the Nazis."

"That is bad. Has he done this often?"

Rudolf lost his head. "Frequently," he said.

"But you said nothing at the time. You made yourself a party to his sedition by your silence."

"I have always been a good friend to Adolf Hitler," said Rudolf, in a breaking voice.

The Captain said: "The Fuehrer is honored. Now, what—else?"

"If you give me time to think . . ."

The Captain said: "No. I do not believe that is necessary. If there was anything that you had to say, obviously, since your life is at stake, you would have said it." He called: "Corporal!"

The Corporal came in and saluted. "Take him in with the others," said the Captain.

Rudolf said: "I beg you not to put me in there with them."

A kind of thunder shook the village. The motorcycles were coming in, the armored cars, lorries, and armored trucks; and in the middle of them all, the great Mercedes-Benz.

A Lieutenant came in. "The Obergruppenfuehrer," he said. "Herr Horner!"

Rudolf saw how the Captain lost something of his suave power, and stood up; and a horrible fear took hold of him. He felt as if two large cold hands had been laid upon his thighs: a great shudder ran through him, a current of cold which swirled and made a vortex at the pit of his stomach. "Sir!" he cried, "Sir, sir!"

The Captain snapped: "Take him away."

Rudolf was dragged out. The Captain looked at his reflection in the glass that covered the photograph of Mr. Hoza's father. Then he drew himself up and went out. The thunder of exhausts stopped. Heels snapped. The door opened. Two officers came in, superlatively elegant and heavily armed, followed by dusty soldiers whose grim faces indicated that they were picked men. Outside, a forest of steel divided itself into an avenue. Along this avenue came a little man. His expensive new uniform hung upon him as upon a little tailor's dummy. Underneath an incongruously rakish cap, a pair of owlish spectacles glittered. The cap-peak shaded a bit of a nondescript nose, an insignificant mustache, and a mouth like a bloodless knife-jab. Behind him strode several high officers. The whole world held its breath: the very trees of the forest seemed to stand stiffly to attention. Every blue-gray sleeve in the room shot out and up and stayed rigid. The little man raised his right arm, too, and then dropped it again. Then he took out a handkerchief, took off his glasses and polished them. He screwed up his eyes as he did so, then hooked his glasses over his ears again.

He seemed to bring with him a coldness, a shadow, and a fear of death. Into that bright morning he carried a feeling of impending night.

He was Heinz Horner.

IX

The Little Black Angel

Having put on his spectacles, Heinz Horner did something which was trivial, but which nobody there ever forgot. With a certain fussy deliberation he took out his watch, flipped it open, peered at it, snapped it shut and put it away.

Then he said: "There is no reason why we should not be finished by tonight."

The Captain conducted him into the other room. Petz, Saxson, and several other officers followed him. The door shut. Everybody waited. Every ear strained. Nobody heard anything.

* * * * *

Heinz Horner hardly ever raised his voice. He had a habit of talking quietly. There had been a time when he had talked like that in order to efface himself: now, his inaudibility was part of his self-assertion. You held your breath to listen to him. You dared not ask him to repeat a word. You hung on his whisper. And when Horner talked so low, who could raise his voice? Therefore the conferences of Heinz Horner were whispered things.

The Captain handed Horner Karel Marek's poem. Horner glanced at it and said: "So?"

"It was suggested that this might be a kind of statement in code——"

"Whoever suggested it is a fool," said Horner. "It is——" His voice took on a certain pedagogic ring: he might have been explaining the rudiments of literature to a junior class: "—a kind of poem, a literary conceit, translatable as faintly subversive in tone, but completely insignificant. Now, what is it you were trying to tell me about two concealed people who ran away, or disappeared, leaving . . . nightdresses I think you said? Leaving some articles of lingerie behind them? What is this again?"

"A nephew, a student, nephew of this schoolteacher, together with his adopted daughter: they seem to have left hurriedly just before our men arrived."

Horner said: "They cannot have gone far. Have you sent anybody to look for them?"

"No, Herr Obergruppenfuehrer."

"It does not matter very much," said Horner. "You see they can't get away. They can't possibly

[103]

get away. Has there been anything at all in the way of information?"

Very eagerly the Captain said: "A man called Svatek is said to be hoarding arms in his house. He is also said to be hoarding money."

Horner replied, gently and soothingly: "It doesn't matter."

The Captain raised his eyebrows. "It doesn't matter at all," said Horner.

"There are allegations against the Mayor, also."

"So? Well, let there be allegations against the Mayor. It doesn't matter."

The Captain stole a glance at Petz. Petz, nervously biting his lip, was looking at Saxson, upon whose face there was a faint inscrutable smile.

At the back of Horner's throat something clicked. He was laughing. Then he said: "This serves several useful functions. It is, I trust, quite obvious to everybody present that this serves several useful functions. Several. It has provided something in the nature of a battle-practice for unblooded troops. It has also provided a species of experiment in synchronization." He looked at his watch again. "Quite a large machine went into motion quite smoothly and worked to time. This is worth knowing." He shut his watch. "Much more important, it is going to provide a valuable demonstration, a very salubrious example, to the whole of Czechoslovakia. Gentlemen, there

are various ways of dealing with Terror. It is alleged that Terror is a useless and outmoded weapon.
This may or may not be so. But one thing is certain,
and that is, that Terror has a certain value. It at-
tracts a certain romantic sympathy to the terrorist
together with publicity to his cause. Of course, gentlemen, the best possible antidote to Terror is, re-
moval of the cause of it. The next best, let us say,
lies in removing the value of it. One proves that the
game is not worth the candle; and just as one may
apply Counter Revolution to Revolution, so one may
apply Counter Terror to Terror. You may regard
this, gentlemen, as an essay in Counter Terror—a
conclusive practical example. You will find, I am
convinced, that Counter Terror can be unarguably
effective if one is prepared to carry it through to the
bitter end and to fulfill—more than fulfill—any
threat one may be called upon to utter. It is alleged
that one cannot possibly wipe out a whole nation.
Be this as it may. It is one's duty to indicate that
one is fully prepared to do so if necessary.

"The Obergruppenfuehrer and General of Police
von Bertsch was assassinated. We have traced the
assassin to this locality. There is not very much
doubt that somewhere in these three parishes the
man is concealed who shot von Bertsch. Very good.
We must proceed to make such an example of Dudicka as will put an end for ever to the Terror in

Czechoslovakia. The Czechs are a beaten people. A beaten people always throws up its martyrs in the cause of Nationalism. Nothing is more simple, or in some cases more delightful, than martyrdom. Now we, gentlemen, are going to demonstrate that in raising a hand against the Reich a man does not merely risk his own trivial life. He does not only risk the life of his wife, or the lives of members of his family. He places in jeopardy the lives of his entire community. His entire community. We regard his village, his town, even his city, as we regard a puddle which has bred a dangerous mosquito. We pour paraffin on such a puddle. We burn out such a community. Calmly, gentlemen, cleanly and scientifically.

"The matter becomes impersonal as the condemnation of a criminal in a court of law. Do I make myself clear?"

Everybody said *yes*.

"It is established," said Saxson, "that the motorcycle was found outside this village."

"Quite," said Horner. "And now this is what you must do. You must separate into three separate groups the entire population of Dudicka.

"In one place I want every man from the age of seventeen upwards.

"In another, every woman from sixteen upwards.

[106]

"Children up to the age of three may stay with their mothers.

"All children, males from three to seventeen years old, and females from three years old to fifteen are to be segregated in a third place. Clear, Colonel Petz?"

"Clear, Herr Obergruppenfuehrer," said Colonel Petz.

Horner looked at the Captain, who stiffened. Horner said: "I do not think that you need to bother your head about isolated units of population that may have straggled into the woods. An unbreakable cordon of men has been thrown around Dudicka."

The Captain clicked his heels.

"Major Haubt!"

Major Haubt stood to attention.

Horner said: "The walnut orchards here are very old and, as timber, of very great value. That is quite clear, I hope?"

Major Haubt said that it was perfectly clear: "I propose if the Obergruppenfuehrer pleases, to take them down first of all and float them down the stream."

Horner said: "And you, Major Mahler? Are you quite prepared?"

Major Mahler said: "Captain Pommer is making a survey at this moment: I shall be ready to go to work the very moment the Obergruppenfuehrer pleases to give the word."

Horner took out a fountain pen, unscrewed it, fitted the cap on to the base. He used only the finest kind of nib.

He took out a notebook with a black leather cover, and tested his pen-nib on his left thumb-nail. "Oh, by the way," he said, "I have my eye on Pommer, and I want a report on him after this affair. I believe that he is a young man deserving of promotion." Then Horner began to make arithmetical notes in almost microscopic figures on one corner of a page in his notebook. It was easy to see that this was a man who, from his earliest years, was accustomed to watching the cost of notepaper and ink. Everybody was quiet. Then, after a few minutes, Horner said:

"I should say: Metal, et cetera, one lorry: tools and heavy implements, et cetera, one lorry; livestock, one lorry; women and children, three lorries, large, covered."

He added: "This is not a picnic. It will not hurt them to stand a little. By the way, there is one thing that should not be forgotten. Major Mahler, you had better dig me a trench. The dimensions of it I will leave to you."

Mahler clicked his heels.

"Major Haubt," said Heinz Horner, "yours will

be the longest job. You had better get to work now."

Haubt saluted and went out.

"You too, Colonel Petz," said Heinz Horner. When Petz had gone Horner said to Saxson: "All goes well on your side I suppose."

Saxson, with his confident smile, replied: "In an affair of this sort, my principle is: small firing squads and plenty of them, and let everybody have a taste."

"Psychologically sound," said Horner, polishing his spectacles.

X

Prelude to Promotion for Pommer

It was scarcely necessary for Captain Johann Pommer to receive the word of command before he went to work. He was a young man of intensely active conscience. His Commanding Officer said: "Collect scrap."

Pommer went to work.

He had considered, with infinite care, the metallic possibilities of Dudicka. Dudicka was a village, a village like every village in the world. One might have said that it concealed no iron. But Captain Pommer knew everything that was hidden in Dudicka, from precious to base metals.

In his breast pocket he had a notebook. On about the third or fourth page of this notebook there was a list. It ran somewhat as follows:—

There is a lead roof to the church.

This is a Catholic village: there are numerous Christs.

They go in for iron stoves. There must be seventy or eighty stoves in Dudicka.

The population is agrarian. Therefore, there will be a considerable quantity of steel as used for plow-coulters, hoes, scythes, sickles, spades, etc., etc.

Tools: picks, shovels, etc., etc.

They have no electricity and no gas. They employ lamps. Most of these lamps are of brass. Each lamp involves about two or three pounds of brass. Granted that there are ninety lamps in the village. There is, therefore, perhaps 150 kilos of brass.

150 kilos of brass makes . . . (?) . . . shell-cases.

Precious metal. Rings, wedding, gold.

Rings, wedding, silver.

Watches, etc.

Personal jewelry, etc.

Underneath this he had written the following words:—

Absolutely nothing must be overlooked.

Then there was a commentary:—"Two or three grams of lead may be a death warrant for an enemy of the Reich. Therefore, to permit any gram of lead to escape one's notice is to reprieve one whom the Reich has condemned."

Jesuses. Above the figure, there is usually a metal

scroll. I.N.R.I. Query: is it worth while in every case to remove these?

Knives: separate these. Steel. Knives and razors. These are valuable.

For the want of a nail the shoe was lost; for the want of a shoe the horse was lost; for the want of a horse the rider was lost; for the want of a rider the battle was lost; for the want of the battle the kingdom was lost . . . And all for the want of a horse-shoe nail!

Zinc. Nickel. No single gram must be wasted.

*   *   *   *   *

Captain Johann Pommer knew, more by instinct than by reason, that he was due for promotion. He was aware that his value depended upon his exactitude. He knew that he had the same kind of use as the rake of a croupier. He was a collector of scrap metal. It was necessary that no scrap escaped him. He found himself thinking of locks, keys, bolts, penknife blades, spoons, forks, and tin tacks. He told himself that if he could manage to scrape out of Dudicka every shred of metal, leaving not even a nail, he would have achieved a certain vital function. He had been looking forward to some such job as this: it was he who had protested against the leaving of metal casters on the feet of armchairs at the period of the destruction of another village. There was, about Pommer, something a little ridiculous. His men hated him: there was a womanish calculation about him. He knew the whereabouts of every nail. He could calculate the number of screws essential to a piece of furniture. Once he had been on the Forestry Commission. Then, a Corporal had said: "Never let Pommer give your kid a lollipop, because the time will come when he will ask for the stick."

* * * * *

He began in the middle of the village. The church had a roof of lead. He told his Lieutenant: "In this roof there is the wherewithal for perhaps two hundred thousand rounds of ammunition . . . I refer, of course, to small-arms ammunition."

He looked at the mutilated Christ inside. A copperplate engraved with the inscription: *Jesus of Nazareth, King of the Jews,* was nailed above the stricken head. The sententious Pommer said: "You must bear in mind that that plate contains copper enough to make cases for about one hundred rounds of ammunition . . . or, perhaps, one hundred and fifty rounds of tommy-gun ammunition."

He saw the candlesticks, three of which were made of brass, and two of which were of silver. He said: "I trust that you recognize the significance of brass, and that you do not ignore the importance of silver."

[113]

He had worked out the weight of studs in a peasant's boots. He had calculated the value of hinges in the door of a hut. He knew precisely how many shell-cases could be made out of the lamps of nine working men's huts. He was aware of the scientific-instrument value of every chip-diamond in a poor girl's engagement ring. He was a statistician: he had converted used contraceptives into terms of tires for lorries, and had reduced the fornication of a nation to terms of mileage. To him, the acquisitions of a family could be spoken of only as rounds of ammunition for the Third Reich.

Before anybody knew that anything really dreadful was going to happen to Dudicka, Captain Pommer had started to strip the village naked. He began to remove the roof of the church in strips of one meter wide. He organized heaps of metal. Lead was laid next to the church roof. Copper went with the scroll that had hung over the head of Christ. Brass followed the candlesticks. Precious metals, he decided, were to go into two wooden boxes. Tempered steel was thrown into a cart . . . scythe-blades, sickles, reaping hooks, tableknives, cart-tires, harrows, and small tools such as saws, chisels, picks, and hammers.

Pommer felt that much depended on his organization of this collection of scrap. He even evolved a tiny heap which, mentally, he labeled: *Soft, heavy.*

This heap consisted of one antimony cigarette box cast in a Chinese style with a representation of a five-clawed dragon on the lid.

Pommer proposed to leave nothing unspecified and uncollected. He set aside tools of wrought iron or steel that had wooden handles, including small screwdrivers, brad-awls, corkscrews, and pocketknives.

If he was doubtful of the nature of a metal he placed it in a heap marked merely with a sign of interrogation: on this heap he threw the tops of soda-water siphons, and several vases which had been sold as bronze.

Colonel Petz had not yet sorted the people of Dudicka into heaps. They thought, simply, that Captain Pommer was collecting metal again for Hitler. It had happened before. It had been necessary for them to save their knives and bladed tools with a certain desperation.

But when Colonel Petz, accompanied by ten very big soldiers, began to sort out the population, there fell upon the village of Dudicka a hideous sense of doom.

Yes, it was only when Colonel Petz—that dried-up, bone-tired, dead-weary man—made his rounds; it was only then that the people of Dudicka felt disposed to say a prayer or two, for they felt that they were in the grip of irresistible and incalculable forces.

[115]

XI

Colonel Petz Decants a Population

Nᴏᴛ ꜰᴀʀ ꜰʀᴏᴍ Dᴜᴅɪᴄᴋᴀ there was an old dump of scrap metal, not worth collecting, for it was eaten up with rust. Over this scattered heap of debris the wild birds and the wind had carried seeds. There were flowering shrubs among the grass. The metal had been thrown down in a hollow. The hollow was full of broken things, all red with rust. Here lay strange fragments of smashed machines . . . immense cogwheels with broken teeth, twisted girders deeply marked by fire, burst boilers between the plates of which little weeds sprouted, splintered pipes of fantastic girth, coils, tubes—the guts of behemoth. Ants crawled in the crevices of half-buried stoves. A blasted dynamo, disintegrating in a chaos of rotted wire, sprouted little yellow blossoms. A music stand hung, quite still, from the top of a sapling which had grown under it and lifted it five feet in the air. A section of a vast drainpipe lay against the disemboweled mechanism of a colossal clock, which once had boomed the passing of time from the top of a tower. Everything was too rusty to be worth the trouble of melting. There were railway lines, bent like the tendrils of creeping plants; part of a locomotive falling to red powder; the iron framework of a piano; huge screws, flattened saucepans, connecting-rods which met nothing, taps dropping to green dust, cisterns, part of a steam roller, portion of a headless iron statue of a nameless woman, a bit of a steel tower ripped up like an old collar . . . the indescribably desolate detritus of an iron age, rotting and rusting away, disappearing beyond hope of salvation, going back to the earth flake by flake. Soon, the soil would digest it, and all these things which so much agony and sweat had evolved would be gone—would disappear as if they had never been. Thus the earth gulps back the work of man.

This dump, all that remained of some dead proposition concerning the manufacture of steel, formed a background to the isolated house of the Kafka family. It was Mrs. Kafka who had just given birth to twins. In normal times, happier times, the village might have chosen the occasion of this double birth as an excuse for some merrymaking. Roman Kafka owned the tobacco shop. He was nearly forty years old, and had been married for twenty years to one of the daughters of the innkeeper. Kafka and his wife had loved each other very dearly. Her name was Teresa: she was a beautiful slender woman of about thirty-seven, with gray eyes and a gentle face framed in heavy dull-blond hair. They had wanted children, but somehow Teresa Kafka remained childless. After the Occupation she became pregnant: Roman handled her like infinitely precious porcelain. But the child was never born. It miscarried. Less than a year later she became pregnant again, and then it seemed that nothing in the world could shake loose the fruit of her womb. She survived an attack of food-poisoning and an accidental fall. The hidden child "was determined to be born," as Roman said. "He has dug himself in. He is a proper Kafka. He has a grip." Roman Kafka was nicknamed "Pincers" on account of his big, phenomenally-powerful handgrip. Teresa grew huge, taut as a ripe fruit. The midwife, Mrs. Pliva, said that there were at least two children there; possibly three. She was a formidable old woman, wise in obstetrical diagnostics, famous for her uncanny intuitions. Once, when the Mayor's wife was two months' pregnant, Mrs. Pliva had said: "It is in the pipe." She meant the Fallopian tube. No doctor could have guessed this, but it was true: Mrs. Hoza nearly died.

At the inn, Roman Kafka became a bore. He led

every conversation round to his wife and her preg-
nancy. If anybody said: "I have torn my hat,"
Roman would say: "And speaking of hats reminds
me of heads: Mrs. Pliva—did I tell you?—says she
distinctly felt two heads." If the talk was of money,
Roman Kafka found an opportunity to say: "Some
people are slow payers, but sure. For example, Teresa did not give me a child for twenty years, and
now she is going to give me two at once." Or Re-
ligion: "Speaking of the Trinity—Mrs. Pliva says
there may be triplets there." Or haystacks: "Mrs.
Pliva says she has never seen a woman of such a
size as my Teresa. Did I tell you there are going to
be twins?" Or cows: "My Teresa makes more milk
than anybody else ever made in Dudicka. But she'll
need it. Have I told you that there are going to be
two little mouths?" Once he had a fight with the
dour and obstinate Elias Svatek. "They will be
boys," said Roman.

"And I say they are girls."

"Why should they be girls?"

"Why shouldn't they be girls?"

"I say they're boys."

"What do you know about it?"

"Aren't they *mine?*"

"Yes, but can you *see* them?"

"No, but why *shouldn't* they be boys?"

"Well, why *should* they be boys?"

[119]

Roman lost his temper and said: "You are a pig-headed idiot."

Elias, also angry, said: "You are a fool, with your twins!"

"You leave my boys alone!"

"Or girls," said Elias. "Most likely girls."

"You Svateks are girl-mad. Look at your brother Rudolf!"

"And what about your Uncle Prokop who got both the Birek sisters into trouble?" shouted Elias.

"And what about *your* sister? Why did she go into service in Prague all of a sudden?" yelled Roman.

Elias replied: "You shut up about her. There were some pretty funny stories about your sister, if it comes to that."

"Better than the stories about your mother's brother, Elias!"

Then the fight started. Roman and Elias were separated. Roman's lip was cut: Elias had a black eye. When Roman got home Teresa asked him what had happened. "That fool of an Elias was making remarks about our two boys."

"And say they are girls?" asked Teresa.

"Why girls?"

"Girls are born, Roman, like everybody else. *I* was born."

[120]

Roman said, with infinite magnanimity: "I will give way to you in this, Teresa. One boy, one girl."

"I should like a girl," said Teresa.

"No, what pleases you pleases me: I hope they are both girls."

"For your sake, Roman, let them both be boys, because I only want to give you pleasure."

"Well, Teresa, for your sake I hope they are both girls."

The men who loitered to talk in Kafka's little tobacco shop found themselves involved in nothing but obstetrical discussion. Then Mrs. Pliva came. The powerful and impulsive Kafka wanted to stop the birds' singing and the rustling of the trees. He shouted to the sparrows: "Shut up your screaming!" The labor was long and difficult. Roman groaned louder than Teresa, wringing his hands. Mrs. Pliva threw water over him. At last the twins were born. They were both boys. All that Roman Kafka could say was: "They're very small"—in a faint voice. Mrs. Pliva snapped: "What do you expect? Plowhorses? What do you think Teresa is? A river in which you fish? What do you want me to do—throw them back because they are small?"

"Don't you dare," said Roman. Teresa was asleep. He galloped on his thick legs to the inn, roared for beer all around, and said to Elias Svatek, in a calm and complacent voice: "When *I* say *I'm* going to have *boys, I* have *boys!"* And burst into joyous tears.

They decided to name the boys Jan and Prokop. Before the twins were six hours old Roman had laid plans covering the first twenty years of their lives. Teresa was deep in a sleep as soft and healing as ointment. By her side two screwed-up purple faces protruded from two white bundles: the boys were exhausted, too—one cannot be born without a struggle.

"Six hours old!" said Roman, when they woke up. "And listen to those voices! Like steam whistles! I am going to save up some money and buy them Hoza's orchard. They shall both be married on the same day. Listen! By God and the Devil—one of them spoke! He said *Roman!* Strike me dead if I didn't hear him! Look at them—they understand every word I say!"

But before they had lived thirty-six hours, their father was standing, sullen and silent, in the Mayor's house with the others who had been brought in for questioning; and Petz's men were on their way to the tobacco shop.

*   *   *   *   *

Teresa was saying: "I thought I heard people coming in this morning, Mrs. Pliva."

"It's nothing," said the midwife.

"Where is Roman?"

"He's gone to the Mayor's house to help with something, some inquiry, the Devil knows what nonsense. It's nothing."

"Is everything all right, Mrs. Pliva?"

"Do you want to turn your milk?"

"I'm worried."

"That is not the way to have children. If you worry you'll give them bellyaches."

"They have flat noses, Mrs. Pliva. Will they grow up with flat noses?"

"They will have noses just like yours, straight, neither too big nor too small." The midwife's face was wrinkled and brown, glossy as well-worn leather, and her pale gray eyes were round and clear as raindrops. She was liked for her good heart and feared for her unkind tongue. Mrs. Pliva was of an irascible temperament: she was not far from the truth when she said: "I have smacked half the bums and all the faces in Dudicka in my time." Now, she was holding her nerves on a short rein. Between words she listened. There was an engrossed detachment in her face—you have seen that look in the eyes of doctors who are touching, feeling, searching for something. Mrs. Pliva had the edge of her hand on the belly of the morning: she knew that the day was going to bring forth monstrosities.

"Sleep again now," she said.

"No, let me stay awake a little longer." Teresa held the midwife's hand. Their eyes met.

"Very well. But you ought to sleep and get strong quickly."

"Mrs. Pliva," said Teresa, suddenly. "When you were a little girl did you use to throw Death into the water on the fourth Sunday in Lent?"

"Naturally."

"Did you cut down a little tree and tie a doll to it, dressed in white? And go about the village singing: *We carry Death out of Dudicka. . . . We bring Summer into Dudicka?* We used to."

"I come from Tabor," said Mrs. Pliva. "It's a little bit different there. At Tabor we used to throw Death down into the water from a high rock. And in other places they burn a straw doll and sing: *Now we carry Death out of the village, the New Summer into the village: Welcome dear Summer, Little green corn.* It is a lot of child's play. Why do you ask?"

"I don't know. I just remembered it. Mrs. Pliva, how many children have you had?"

"About six." The midwife listened.

"Are they——"

"Five are dead. One, the eldest, is in America. I've heard nothing from him for three years: he may be President of the United States for all I know. Three I lost in the last war. The other two just died like other people, of diphtheria."

[124]

"Did you like being married?" Teresa, half-dozing, closed her eyes.

"Like it? Why, what is there to like about it? Everybody has got to be married." Mrs. Pliva sat tensely.

"Were you afraid at first?"

"Me? Afraid? Of *Pliva?* No, he was afraid of me. Men are like that. They talk big, oh yes! But when the lamp goes out . . . ha!"

". . . *Death swims in the water . . . Summer visits us with red eggs . . .*" murmured Teresa, falling asleep. Then she opened her eyes again and said: "I wish Roman would come back." She was awake again. "Mrs. Pliva, Roman is a sillier baby than these two here. Do you know that he is already talking about finding them wives? Wives! And do you know what he said? He said: 'What a pity I had to hand in my guns: that little light Austrian gun would have been just the thing for our boys to learn with.' "

Mrs. Pliva stood up. She heard men marching. "Wait a moment," she said, and walked to the door. A dozen of Petz's picked infantrymen were coming. A young officer marched in front of them. The midwife saw, then, that from every point similar groups were approaching other houses. She said to the officer: "Keep your men quiet, you!"

"What's that?" he said.

[125]

"Shut up! There's a woman in here who's just had twins."

"Congratulations," said the officer, and pushed Mrs. Pliva aside. Two noncommissioned officers followed him into Teresa's bedroom. Mrs. Pliva, buzzing like a hornet, placed herself between the soldiers and the bed. Teresa, clutching her babies, stared at them with wide, terrified eyes. "You are to come with me," said the officer.

"Why, you damned idiot," said Mrs. Pliva, "can't you see she's just had twins?"

"You are to come with me all the same."

"She can't walk, you fool!"

"You'd better be civil, old woman!"

Teresa could not speak. Mrs. Pliva, holding down her anger and her terror, said: "Look. Be sensible. How can she move? Only a few hours ago—twins! Look at them, see for yourself! If you want her—well, look: can she run away?"

"I am sorry: you must both come with me." The officer looked down at Teresa. "You must pull yourself together and come with me. It is an order. You must bring the children with you. You too, old woman."

Mrs. Pliva shrieked: "And if she was your mother?"

"Orders are orders," said the officer.

"It'll kill her if you make her try to walk."

"She must try."

"But what is this for?"

"I have orders to take you to the church. Every woman in Dudicka, and all children in arms."

"But why? Why? Good God, why? What for?"

"It's an order. If she doesn't come immediately, she'll be dragged there. It's an order."

Mrs. Pliva was shocked into silence. "What kind of men *are* you?" she whispered, at last.

"All right. Come on," said the officer, and grasped Teresa's wrist.

"You dare!" screamed the midwife. She picked up a chamberpot. The officer paused. The ten riflemen and the two sub-machine-gunners fell back half a pace. Then an ox-faced Corporal said: "Permission to speak, sir? Four men could carry her on the featherbed, one holding each corner."

"Right. Hurry up."

In the street women were shrieking and men were shouting.

Four riflemen handed their rifles to their neighbors and grasped the featherbed. It was Teresa's dowry! It contained the hoarded goose down of forty years. "Hup!" said the Corporal. Mrs. Pliva watched, choked with rage. Teresa lay, clutching the twins: they both began to cry together. She wept helplessly. The soldiers dragged the sagging, swaying bundle out into the street. Mrs. Pliva walked

beside them, holding Teresa's hand, saying: "There
. . . there . . . there . . ." They reached the church.
More soldiers than Mrs. Pliva could count were
driving women and young children through the doorway. The women of Dudicka went in, huddled together, looking back in anger and fear. Some wept;
some screamed; some were silent. One of them
reached out and tried to scratch a soldier's face. He
drove the butt of his rifle into her bosom. Above
everything rose a wailing of children.

XII

Echo

Now Duda was watching this scene. Duda, half-brother to the twilight and friend of things that hide, had pressed back into Max's hand the colored glass marble, and, with a sidling run, disappeared into the shadows. It could not be said that Duda made an exit: he went out as a candle goes out. A flicker, and then darkness where he had stood. So he watched, and saw what was happening in the village, while Max and Anna waited in the cave.

Anna said: "Max, I am cold."

"Dare we make a fire, a very little fire?" said Max. "Yes, I think so. Look, let's go over to the narrower part, there. We can make a tiny fire with some of these dry branches; it won't smoke much if we pick dry branches, Anna. A tiny little fire will be enough: it isn't really very cold . . . only dark . . ." He was picking up twigs.

"I'd rather be with you in the dark and the cold, than with anybody else in the sunlight," said Anna.

"It won't always be dark and cold," said Max. He dragged the nest Duda had made to the mouth of the narrow cave that echoed. "Only a little way up there, everything is warm and bright."

Right! . . . Right! . . . said the echo, from the bowels of the cave.

He made a small fire, took off his coat and put it over Anna's shoulders. He felt something heavy in his pockets. It was the meat, bread and onion Karel Marek had given him. He said:

"You haven't breakfasted."

Fasted . . . Fasted . . . said the echo. But Max and Anna did not notice it.

Anna shook her head. Max said: "Here is some bread and meat."

Eat . . . Eat . . . said the echo.

Anna and Max were crouching on the bed of branches that Duda had laid down. Her head was on Max's shoulder. Suddenly, he felt something wet on his cheek. She was weeping. At first she wept silently; then she sobbed, and the echoes sobbed with her. The stone walls sobbed, the buried darkness sobbed.

"Dearest!" said Max.

Rest . . . Rest . . . Rest . . . said the echo.

[130]

Anna whispered: "I can't help thinking of the daybreak."

Ache . . . Ache . . . said the echo.

Max replied, very gently: "Yes, and now we are in a hole underground in the dark; but we'll find somewhere."

Where? . . . Where? . . . asked the echo.

"The day began . . . so splendid . . ." said Anna, weeping.

Ended . . . Ended . . . said the echo, weeping too.

"We'll bring back this dawn somehow," said Max.

"How? . . . How? . . . said the echo.

"Where?" asked Anna.

Air . . . Air . . . said the echo.

There was a silence.

Max said: "There *is* an end in view . . ." He paused.

You . . . You . . . said the echo.

". . . There can be a point in running away, and an end to flight."

Light! . . . Light! . . . said the echo.

"Max, I love you: but I'm afraid of all the time that has to pass before we get where we belong."

Long . . . Long . . . said the echo.

Max held her closer. She cried: "Oh, darling, where will we be before all this is ended?"

Dead . . . said the echo *. . . Dead . . . Dead . . .*

Time passed. Then Duda darted out of the dark-

[131]

ness and stamped the fire out with his feet. He was shaking with fear, sobbing and trembling.

* * * * *

Duda clutched Max's hand "No!" he said, and pointed upwards. "No! Bad! Bad! Bad!"

"What's happening?" asked Max.

"People," said Duda, and clenched his fists and beat the air. "Men. Bad, bad, bad!"

"He means they're beating people," said Max.

Duda held up the fingers of his left hand, grabbed them in his right fist; the imprisoned fingers struggled, but the fist dragged them down into a pocket, thrust them in and held them there. "Church," said Duda.

And he whispered, shuddering: "Mother! Mother!"

To Duda, the word "mother" meant torment, imprisonment, privation, the terror of confinement and the pain of bruises. It was the most terrible word he knew: it made him remember a red face, a red fist, a slamming door, a clicking lock, a darkness and an anguish. "Mother," he said, and hid his face in his hands.

"They are beating people and locking them up in the church," said Max. "I must go back."

"No! No!" cried Duda.

Anna said: "What can you do if you go back?"

[132]

"I don't know, but I must go."

"Then I must come with you."

"No, Anna, you must stay here."

"Max, you don't think that I'm going to let you go away from me now?"

"It would be crazy for you to take the risk."

"Because there is a risk, Max, there is all the more reason why I should come with you. Say you were killed."

"Anna, you don't understand. I am a man, and I should only be killed. But you are a woman, and not only a woman, but the most beautiful woman in Czechoslovakia and the whole world, and so it would not be anything so simple as death for you."

"Nobody on earth could make me stay alive if you were dead."

"Anna, you mark my words, it is easy to talk like that, but life is not a thing that people give up so easily. I have seen it in the hospital in Prague. Even people with cancer want to hold on a little bit longer, because even pain can be better than absolutely nothing at all."

"I do not believe that there will be absolutely nothing at all, Max, and I am going to go with you; and if you make me stay here I shall follow you alone."

"Then I suppose you must come with me," said Max, and smiled. She could just see the whiteness of his teeth in that half-light. Then he said to Duda: "You must show us the way to get back without being seen."

Duda wrung his hands and said: "No. no."

"Yes, Duda."

"Men . . . bad . . ." Duda spread his arms in a wide gesture which said *Men are everywhere*.

Max began to walk back to the mouth of the cave. Anna followed him. But Duda, quick as a weasel, darted in front of him and cautiously pushed aside the thorn-bush that hid the entrance. With a hundred little terrified gestures he pointed. Max looked in the direction indicated by the brown hairy finger. The forest was full of men. Steel glinted between the trees. Hundreds of soldiers, foresters and pioneers, were coming with axes and saws. "What are they going to do?" asked Anna.

Max did not answer this question. He said: "We can't possibly get through."

Duda laid a finger on his lips and cupped a hand at his left ear. Through the clear air there floated a new harsh sound, a sound like a death rattle.

"A saw," said Max, "they are cutting down trees. What for?" Then he said: "We must find another way. If necessary, we will wait until dark."

"Uncle Karel wanted us to wait until it was dark and then try and go away," said Anna.

"Uncle Karel is a saint. But does that mean to say

that I have got to be less than a man? Say anything terrible happened to him, and I had run away! Could I ever look in my shaving mirror again without spitting at myself?"

"Whatever you say is right," said Anna, "always."

They went back. Max paced the floor of the cave under the scintillating dome, biting his nails. Then, suddenly, he stopped dead and cried: "By God!"

"What?" asked Anna.

"There must be another way out of here. Don't you realize that? Don't you realize that there is always a little current of fresh air coming from down there?" Max pointed into the thick darkness of the cave of echoes. "Duda, there, there, you, Duda— have you ever been there?"

"Bad," said Duda, "No, no."

"We are going there," said Max.

Duda writhed beseechingly. Then he went to his little pathetic treasure-house and picked up the yellow china cat with blue eyes and offered it to Max. "No?" he said, with a twisted smile.

"Yes," said Max, and began to pick up pine branches. "We will make torches and see our way. At least we can see if there is another way out."

"Let us go," said Anna.

At this moment they heard a heavy crash in the distance; then another.

"Trees are coming down," said Max. He lit a pine

[135]

branch. It burned with a pale and smoky flame. Another tree fell. "They must be cutting down our walnut forests," said Max; and he added in a tone of bitter incredulity: "I cannot understand such people."

The torch as it flared sent wild shadows dancing in the darkness of the echoing cave. Half to himself, in a sad undertone, Max said: "What is there to defeat such an enemy?"

And the echo, from the bowels of the earth, solemly replied: *Me!*

Then they walked into the cave of echoes.

XIII

A Minor Technical Error

At this moment, guards on the road-block outside Dudicka stopped an enormous camouflaged car driven by a formidable army driver.

The passenger thrust out of the window an angry gray head. He was a gray, grim man, with something of the bulldog in the set of his jaw and the sag of his dewlap. His eyes were bloodshot. He wore a mustache of the out-dated Kaiser Wilhelm pattern. He was fifty years old, but looked sixty. There was authority in his manner, iron in his voice, and arrogance in the cock of his head. A couple of ancient duelling scars marked parallel lines on the left-hand side of his jaw. He carried the ribbon of a decoration.

He roared at the sergeant on guard: "Von Essen, Major, Engineers! Immediate business with the Obergruppenfuehrer! Quick!"

"Your papers, please, Major," said the Sergeant.

"Dung-faced bastard," said von Essen, holding out a pass.

The Sergeant saluted, the car passed through. Major von Essen sat, savagely drumming on his knees with his fingers. He was an irascible man, a disappointed man, an expert in internal combustion engines who had never succeeded in achieving a position beyond that of a mediocre staff officer's. He had birth, intelligence and integrity; but younger men had been promoted over his head. He was thorough, rigid, unshakable; but the tide of affairs had gone over him and left him standing, gray and bitter, like a rock in the sea.

He reached the Mayor's house.

"The Obergruppenfuehrer. I'm Major von Essen. My business is very urgent and private. Quickly."

The Captain clicked his heels, begged him to wait, and reported his arrival to Heinz Horner. Horner said: "Ask Major von Essen what he wants."

The Captain returned to von Essen, who was stamping his feet outside. "The Obergruppenfuehrer has told me to ask you what you want to see him about."

"My business with him is very private and extremely urgent. I can tell it to no one but him. Be so kind as to inform him of this, damned quick!"

"I am sorry," said the Captain, firmly, "but his instructions were very definite."

Von Essen ground his teeth, and then said: "Well, listen." He lowered his voice. "You can tell the Obergruppenfuehrer that there is a mistake concerning the motorcycle. Just tell him that, and add that I will explain fully when I see him."

"Have the goodness to wait, Major von Essen." The Captain went back into Horner's room; came out again and said: "The Obergruppenfuehrer will see you."

"I am obliged and honored," grunted von Essen, scowling. He stamped in, saluted, and stood with his heavy chest thrown out.

"Wait outside, Captain," said Horner. When they were alone he said: "Well, Major von Essen, what is it?"

The Major snapped back: "There seems to have been some silly blunder somewhere."

"Explain, please," said Horner.

"It concerns the motorcycle alleged to have been ridden by the murderer, which was found near this village."

"Yes?"

"I have examined it."

"Yes?"

"Not that it needed much examination. The machine that they found here could not possibly have

[139]

been the one upon which the murderer rode the other night. In fact, nobody could possibly have ridden the machine for years. A casual glance would convince a purblind imbecile that it could not have been ridden."

"I am afraid," said Horner, in his deadly little prim voice, "I am afraid, Major von Essen, that I must ask you to adopt a more respectful tone when you speak to me."

"I humbly beg your pardon," said von Essen, saluting. "But whoever it was that informed you concerning this motorcycle was either a rogue or a fool. The model they found here is mere scrap iron. It is thick with rust. It is completely worn-out. It is good for nothing at all, not even fit for melting down. I cannot understand how such an error was made."

"What you are telling me is this: that the motorcycle found near Dudicka was not the machine for which we are looking?"

"Precisely that."

"And why was I not informed of this sooner?"

"As a matter of form the machine was sent to me, for examination. I duly examined it, and prepared a report—that it was an English model, made by Douglas; that it had been in a crash perhaps three years ago, and that certain parts were missing and so on, and so forth. But when I learned that this was the murder-machine, I felt it my duty to come direct to you without wasting time."

Horner took off his glasses and polished them; then put them on again and blinked vaguely at the opposite wall. "You are sure of this," he said.

"Positive."

"Your assistants, for example, confirm this?"

"I am the only competent person who examined it, but in any case there is no earthly doubt."

"And what is current opinion concerning this matter, Major von Essen?"

"There is none: I came straight to you, Herr Obergruppenfuehrer."

"Well," said Horner, "I do not think that it matters a very great deal."

Major von Essen, staring at this little, detestable, bespectacled man, whose every word and gesture seemed to stink of the lower reaches of the civil service, felt a terrible desire to slap him in the face. He said: "I beg pardon?"

"I said, I do not think that it matters a very great deal."

"But . . . please forgive me . . . I hurried here to prevent a mistake, an . . . an . . . error . . . a . . . a . . . miscarriage of justice, sir! Pardon me, but I don't quite understand!"

"It is not necessary for you to understand, Major von Essen. It is not for a soldier to understand,

Major von Essen. A soldier obeys, he obeys without question, without understanding. Unless, of course, he has the gift of understanding, Major von Essen. Where is your report?"

Major von Essen handed Horner an envelope. Horner took it, and placed it on the desk in front of him. "You may go," he said.

"Have I permission to say a word?" Major von Essen said.

"Be very brief."

"I trust that I have, at least, arrived in time to save these peasants from an unmerited punishment?"

"Leave the room, Major von Essen, and wait outside."

Von Essen choked, saluted, and went out. The Captain came in. Heinz Horner was playing with a pencil. He said: "Captain, how long have you been in the Army?"

"Seven years."

"Naturally, you have ambitions?"

"Yes, Herr Obergruppenfuehrer."

"I am thinking, Captain, of having you promoted almost immediately to the rank of Major, with the possibility of even further promotion in a short time."

"Oh, Herr Obergruppenfuehrer, I hope I shall prove myself worthy——"

"First of all, Captain, a little intelligence test . . ." Horner looked down at the envelope containing von Essen's report, and up again at the Captain. "What pistol is that you are carrying, Captain?"

"A 9 mm. Mauser."

"How does it work?"

"One pulls back the bolt by means of the ribbed wings at the back. This cocks the hammer and lets the magazine platform rise . . ."

"I see you know how to use it."

"Yes, Herr Obergruppenfuehrer."

"Is Major von Essen still waiting?"

"Yes, he is still waiting."

Horner drew a ring round the name of von Essen written on the envelope, and blinked at the Captain. "Captain, Major von Essen is a man who has out-lived discretion and usefulness, and is therefore an enemy of the Reich . . . Well?"

The Captain drew himself up to his considerable height and clicked his heels.

"In the best regulated organizations, accidents will happen," said Horner.

"Especially with firearms," said the Captain, and he saluted and went out.

Horner sat, his eyes almost closed. He was sensitive to sudden noises. Perhaps thirty seconds later he heard the bang of a Mauser, slightly muffled. He went to the door and opened it. In the other room, the Captain was standing with an expression of blank dismay on his face. Major von Essen was sitting in a chair, with his head hanging forward. Having heard the shot nine or ten guards came in. The Captain said: "It is a mystery to me how this happened . . . I have never known it to happen before . . . my pistol went off while it was still in the holster. I was standing beside this poor gentleman and the bullet seems to have hit him somewhere in the head."

"We will look into all this later," said Horner, and then went back into his room. Nobody said a word. A few minutes later Horner called the Captain. The little man was polishing his glasses. In an ashtray in front of him lay the ashes of some burned paper gently crackling. Horner said: "It is a great pity that people find it so difficult to realize that, in this new state of things, there is absolutely no room at all for imbecilities belonging to a dead tradition. It is Dudicka that is chosen to provide a warning and an example to Bohemia and Moravia. One Slav village . . . another Slav village . . . what difference can that make? Well, von Essen has proved, and paid for his lack of intelligence; and you, my friend, have proved, and shall be rewarded for, your astuteness. You may rest assured of your majority; and of a colonelcy in the course of time . . . as long as you realize that your surest guarantee of long life and continued prosperity is your absolute discretion."

The Captain saluted. Horner said: "I shall keep my eye on you."

The Captain thrilled with joy and with terror.

"Now, be so good as to shut the windows. The villagers seem to be making a lot of unnecessary noise."

XIV

Unnecessary Noise

It was a cry of women who had lost hope, an outcry unendurably forlorn. There are no words that can describe such a sound; when sadness so expresses itself it is beyond words. The Captain, closing the windows, remembered a scene of desolation: when he was a boy he worked, for a little while, on a ship; and one day the ship touched some Godforgotten point in the Artic circle . . . a frozen emptiness, an infinity of jagged black ice under an unending night, through which, from an incalculable distance, came the melancholy moaning of some animal in pain. He remembered this, dismissed it, and slammed the window down.

Saxson remembered an incident in a concentration camp: they had dragged out the Rabbi and his son, and, standing the old man in the cesspool of the prison, ordered him to say some prayers, and when

he refused, a guard drowned him . . . and then the
son suddenly went mad, and threw back his head
and howled in a voice which did not belong to this
world or to any other world.

And back into the mind of Colonel Petz, rising
like a bubble out of a rottenness at the bottom of a
dark pool, came the memory of a bad dream . . .
he was walking along a road—that was all. Only the
road had no beginning and no end, and no perspec-
tive: its appalling length went on and on and on;
and it was of the color of watery moonlight, and
everything else was black; and his mind had shuddered from the prospect of it and he had sat up in
bed, wide awake and drenched in sweat.

Horner had heard such cries before. He had never
considered them except as inevitable in the course
of business. You pulled out a stop—vox humana—
and when you put your foot down, then the organ
squealed. It was natural. It was quite all right. One
simply shut one's window and concentrated on work,
always on work, organization and superorganiza-
tion. He saw his Gestapo as something that could be
perfect, perfect as a snake is perfect. Every man in
it must fit like a rib in a python; it must be co-
ördinated to hang still or move fast; to hide, slide,
strike, encircle, crush, devour, and hide again waiting. In the still, cold brain of Heinz Horner there
was an ideal, one ideal, sharp and frozen and definite

as an icicle. He wanted a perfect world-wide Gestapo. Somewhere in his mind there lingered a fantasy, some memory of a legend of the ice gods. There was a serpent; it wound around the world, gripping it and holding it together for ever. He saw himself as this serpent, tail-in-mouth, pitiless, passionless, a thing in himself, a beginning and an end.

He drew a neat ring around the word *Women* at the head of a list before him.

When Heinz Horner's pencil described an *O*, voices always shrieked.

Well, they were shrieking now.

* * * * *

Colonel Petz was an adroit and intelligent officer. He knew that caution is always necessary, and that even a conqueror must look out for himself, even in a conquered village. So he had segregated the men first of all. This was extremely simple. He had simply ordered every man in Dudicka to report to him at the inn; every male from seventeen years old upward. He said: "There is no need at all to run foolish risks. There is no necessity to give oneself trouble with upheavals. If you separate the women first, the men are bound to attempt something, something or other, no matter what. And always remember that even a Slav, even a slave, can become desperate, and in the hands of a desperate man a coffeepot, a knitting needle, even a feather pillow, can be a dangerous weapon. And watch your backs!" And his eyes, like coals which had burned themselves into his face and turned to ashes, lit up for an instant.

It was as he said; the men, ordered to report, did so. In the past three years they had grown accustomed to being ordered to report . . . for census-taking, for forced labor, or for nothing at all. The Germans were like that. So they dragged themselves out, weary and sullen, to the inn, where their names were checked from a list. Then they were shut up in the big room they all knew so well, the room in which, for the past two hundred years, the men and women of Dudicka had celebrated marriages, births, feast days, and sometimes victories. The innkeeper was locked in with them too, and so was his son, Leopold. The heads of all the families in Dudicka were there—all the Kobras, all the Kafkas, all the Mareks, Svateks, Hozas, Blazeks, everybody. They looked at one another. "What is this for?" men asked.

Roman Kafka said to Elias: "This is all the fault of your bloody brother."

For the first time in the history of Dudicka, Elias Svatek did not immediately quarrel with Roman. He simply said: "If you mean that changeling, that

[149]

bastard called Rudolf Svatek, all right. But he is no brother of mine any more."

"If ever I get the chance I am going to break his back across my knee," said Roman.

And Elias replied: "I'll help you. What kind of blood gets into a man, that he does things like that?"

The Mayor said: "Every man in Dudicka is here except Max Marek and Duda. Karel, where is Max?"

"I don't know."

Roman said: "Well, after all, what can they do to us?"

Leopold, the innkeeper's son, said: "They can take us away, for example, to the labor gang. They could even . . . they can do plenty to us. They can send us away."

"They can't do that," said Roman. "God damn it all, they couldn't send us *away!* Why, God strike me dead, my boys have only just got born! God and the Devil, do you realize that after twenty years Teresa has been and had twins, boys? You remember how we had a fight about it, Elias? Eh? How you cut my lip? Eh? And I blacked your eye?" Roman was pale; his ponderous chest was heaving like water. "No, Leopold, they couldn't possibly do that!"

Somebody said: "It can't be for the labor gangs, because look——" he pointed. Roman saw through the packed crowd the crushed figure of old Blazek lying against the opposite wall. The old man was mumbling to himself. A middle-aged farmer who was standing by him turned to the others and said, with a ghastly smile: "God help him, he is asking for a young roast chicken!"

"Where is Otakar?" asked Elias.

And Leopold replied: "You heard those shots? That was Otakar."

Roman muttered: "As long as they don't do anything to the women, to Teresa, I don't care very much. And the kids. And the kids."

Old Balaban took out of his bosom a wineglass, and said in a far-away voice: "This is all they left me."

"They smashed his glasses."

There was a murmur.

Roman's lips were trembling as he said: "But as long as they don't do anything to the women . . ."

A Sergeant came in and, in a shattering roar trained on a hundred parade grounds, cried: "Where's the priest?"

The priest stood up, an aged and tremulous figure.

"Come here!"

The priest went over to him. The Sergeant said: "You're wanted in the church. Come with me."

Leopold said to Roman: "You are telling me about your twins, Roman! I am supposed to be getting married the day after tomorrow."

"I wonder what they want the priest for," muttered Elias.

There was a silence, an oppressive and ponderous silence which nobody seemed able to break.

Then, in a high-piping voice, vague and quivering, the aged Blazek began to sing:

"Her eyes are like two sapphires . . . Her skin is like blood and milk . . . Her hair is like ripe wheat . . . Her breasts are firm enough to crack a flea on . . . And I am marrying her tomorrow . . ."

"The poor old man, what will he do without Otakar?" asked the innkeeper.

"He can come to my house," said Roman.

"Or mine," said Elias.

"I could find room for him," said Marek.

Roman said: "As long as they don't do anything to Teresa."

And as he said this, there came that dreadful and woebegone wail of women.

*　*　*　*　*

It was Teresa Kafka who needed the priest, but Roman did not know this. Even if he had known there was nothing that he could have done about it.

She was a slender woman, but her dead weight on the featherbed was irksome to the soldiers who were carrying her. Furthermore, they felt that their friends would laugh at them. They wanted to be rid

[152]

of their burden as soon as possible. As soon as they were inside the church they let the featherbed fall. Teresa, clasping the twins, fell two feet and screamed as she hit the floor. This scream was the solo out of which sprang the dismal concerted cry that made men's blood stand still a little later. The twins cried too, and Mrs. Pliva exclaimed sharply in horror, hesitated for a split second, and then instead of flying at the soldier's eyes with her nails as her first impulse dictated, stooped to help Teresa.

All the women of Dudicka were in the church. The Mayor's wife was trying to soothe a little desperate woman who was sobbing herself into hysterics. Etta Hertl, deathly pale and silent, was sitting down, trying to protect her swollen abdomen with her raised knees. Other women were comforting terrified babies, whose thin crying made the air vibrate like a violin string. One girl, still little more than a child, was trying to hide her face in her hands. Her black hair was disheveled; the back of it was gray with dust, and there was dust on the back of her thin blue dress. She was weeping with sharp hiccoughing sobs which caught at the nerves like fishhooks. Her eyes were wide open and tearless.

Mrs. Pliva, stooping over Teresa, suddenly gasped. The featherbed which had been white and dry was now no longer white, but red. The little midwife called: "I must have hot water!" She fumbled in her big linen pocket, found nothing; picked up one of the twins and stripped off his outer covering; ripped it into narrow strips and began, with rapid and skillful fingers, to roll them; snatched the pillow that still remained under Teresa's head, raised her with one wiry arm. A dozen women gathered around her fascinated and fearful.

One look at Teresa's face told Mrs. Pliva that she could do nothing. She said to an officer who was looking on with his hands in his pockets: "Murderer, get your doctor, quick!"

"We haven't got one," he said. "So sorry."

"She has a hæmorrhage. She had just had twins. She has shock. They threw her down. She will die. Get a doctor!" She was busy, all the while, with the woman on the mattress. Two other women were holding the babies. One of the women was holding a baby of her own. She gave her child to her sister, undid her dress, and began to feed the tiny shrieking child of Teresa Kafka; the one Roman meant to call Jan, the first-born. The midwife said: "Shameless, look away, and get your doctor." But she knew that Teresa was dying.

The officer was not of the Army, but of Horner's staff; a young man of culture, popular for his charm and intelligence. He was the proud possessor of a gentle and persuasive voice, and was widely read in

[154]

the philosophies. He said: "My good woman, war is war. Believe me I would help if I could. But there is no doctor."

Mrs. Pliva said, in a heavy voice: "Then get the priest," and she wiped her hands on her apron.

The officer, smiling, said: "I am afraid that we don't travel with a priest either, you know." His voice was full of apology. He moistened his thick lower lip.

Mrs. Pliva said to him: "You murderer, you murderer, would you let a poor girl die without a priest? Isn't it enough to kill her body, when she never did anything to hurt you? Do you want her to die, also, without a *priest?* Then her sins will be on your soul, I warn you, double and many times double, killer!"

The young officer, in the first few years of his life, had been brought up by simple-minded parents who feared God and revered all that which is supposed to appertain to Him. He retained, at the back of his mind, a certain awe for the rites of the Church. He shrugged his shoulders and said to the Sergeant at the door: "Is there a priest in the village?"

Twenty women replied: "Yes! Yes! Yes!"

The officer said: "Well, bring him here and then afterwards you can take him back where he belongs."

So the Sergeant went to get the priest. Mrs. Pliva, with tears running down her face, said: "She is not young any more; she was old to be having her first, and it was twins, and it was hard—I am telling you that it was hard, hard! I did not expect her to come through. And then—women, and then to drag her out and throw her down! As if there was so much blood left in her veins as it was! And what for? What has she done? What do they want to do with her? They could not even use her to play with. They don't need her! They don't want her? Then why? Why? Why? How can such things happen? How can they be? Where is God? Kill men, yes, kill men if you must kill men—but give them at least a chance to be born!"

Teresa opened her eyes and said: "Roman. Tell Roman to come."

The midwife said: "He is coming, he will be here in a minute, a few minutes . . ."

"I feel much stronger now," said Teresa, her eyelids fluttering.

Mrs. Pliva whispered to the officer: "Let her husband at least say good night to her!"

"Absolutely not," said the officer.

Teresa whispered: "We used to go about the village singing: *We carry Death out of Dudicka. . . . We bring Summer into Dudicka. . . .* Is Roman coming?"

Mrs. Pliva replied: "Yes, my darling, he is coming."

[156]

"I shall be up and about again . . . in a week . . ." said Teresa, and then she died.

"You have killed her," said Mrs. Pliva. "Go back to Germany and boast that you are a soldier, dog!"

"Black dog!" said another woman.

Then the priest came, the Sergeant gripping his shoulder. The women were silent. Mrs. Pliva said: "You are too late, Father, she has just died."

The priest tried to speak but no words came out of his mouth. Too large tears crept out of his eyes and ran down his nose. He covered his face with his hands, fragile white hands thickly veined and trembling. The girl who had been sobbing came out of the corner and stood before him. He was a very small man. She was not much smaller than he. She said: "Father."

"My child?"

She said: "I want . . ." Her eyes were fixed and glazed with pain. She walked with difficulty. Her whole body was trembling. The priest laid a hand on her head. She grasped his wrist and said: "I am afraid, Father. I could not help it, Father. I did not want to commit adultery, but *they* made me before they took me away."

The priest, also, began to tremble. Still trembling, he stood upright, strode over to where the officer was standing, raised his hands over his head, and began to say: "In the name of——"

The officer recoiled, said: "Sergeant!"

The Sergeant threw himself forward in three long strides. He was a squat Bavarian, with fists like mallets and the neck of a wrestler. He hit the priest once, on his uplifted chin, with all his strength and weight. The old man's feet left the floor. His head hit it. The senile, fragile skull cracked on the stone like an egg against the edge of a basin.

And the women cried out in agony.

XV

Prelude To a Doom

THE LITTLE GIRL looked down at the dead priest, and up at the Sergeant; then walked slowly backwards as if an invisible hand were pushing her, until the wall stopped her, and then she stood there, staring. The Mayor's daughter, Etta Hertl, rose and put her arms round the child, and said: "My poor little love, and you are Ledvina's daughter!"

Ledvina was a man well-known for his piety, who had disappeared into some barbed-wire hell for saying that God was greater than Hitler. Her mother was dead. She lived in the houses of strangers, making herself as useful as she could. Her name was Maria.

Etta said: "In the last three years the world has gone mad. There has been nothing but misery, and misery, and misery. Sit down next to me." Etta Hertl resembled her mother in her strength and calmness.

She saw that the child, Maria, was thawing; that soon, the horror of what had happened would come back into her numbed mind with all the agony of blood returning into a frozen limb; with pain, with shame, and an intolerable impotent rage. But what could she say? She said: "Soon it will be forgotten, you will forget it. Try not to think of it. It is finished, over, done. These people are not men, they are something else. A dog bit you, a big mongrel dog . . . a pig tried to eat you, a filthy wild pig . . . God will punish them, my little one, so now just shut your eyes for a moment and put your head here . . . just here . . . and try to keep still for a minute, just a minute."

Maria wept.

Mina Petera, the girl who was betrothed to the innkeeper's son, said: "Etta, what are they going to do to us? If they do this to a child, what will they do to us? What will they do to us?"

Etta replied: "I don't know, Mina. I don't even know why we're here, except that some German was killed, and we are blamed for it."

Mrs. Pliva said: "And what is going to happen to these two innocent babies?" She was holding one of the twins. Then she said, as firmly as she could: "Women, any of you that have milk must give these orphans some of it . . . poor things, poor little things, and their poor father . . . he nearly went mad, the silly man, and started to talk about teaching them how to shoot, and fish, and finding them wives, and saving up enough money to buy them an orchard. What will happen now?"

In a quivering voice Mina Petera said: "But they don't understand—Leopold and I are going to be married the day after tomorrow! Etta! Tell them that! That's right, Etta, you tell them that! If you tell them they'll listen! Mrs. Hoza, you're the wife of the Mayor, you tell them! They don't know that Leopold and I are going to be married the day after tomorrow! That's it! If somebody tells them . . ."

"Then what?" asked Mrs. Pliva. "Do you see what they did to Teresa Kafka? Expect nothing, child."

"Mrs. Pliva, you tell them!"

"Child, child, nothing has happened to you yet, and if the very worst happens you will only have lost something you never really had. But look at Teresa, look at little Maria, and Etta here . . . be like Etta, Mina Petera! I tell you that Etta is as full of troubles and sorrows as an egg is full of meat. What is going to happen to her little boy, seven years old and with nobody to guide him? And the next one? Yes, when I was a girl, I saw nothing but my own troubles too. But do you see what Etta is holding there; do you see what she is carrying? I had an appointment to be ready for a call from Etta the end

[161]

of the month after next. And what happened to her
husband, Josef? It was worse than anything happening before the wedding. They had already been
married eight years, they were no longer two different people. Etta and Josef were like one person: he
thought what she thought, and she thought what he
thought, and there was no way of pulling them apart
without tearing their hearts in two. And what happened? They took him away to work and they killed
him somewhere——God knows where——somewhere in some German den of slaves and murderers.
Nobody knows how they killed him. Nobody saw
his dead body. Nothing has happened to you yet,
Mina."

"But . . . if you tell them . . ."

Mrs. Hoza laid a calm hand on her head and said:
"Mina, there is no use telling them anything, no use
at all, not the slightest use in the world! I thought
at first that they were people, bad people, but people. Well, they are not people. And they do not regard us as people. Do you know what they say? I
have heard it said a lot of times. *Slaven sind
Sklaven*. Slavs are slaves. They will treat a dog
much better than they would treat one of us. Well,
they conquered us. I don't know how. I know now
that it would have been better if we had died before
they conquered us. Mina, expect nothing. Keep your
eyes on heaven and your faith in God. Their time

will come. But until it does . . ." She shrugged her shoulders, and added: "But then again, I am an old woman and I have had my life, but you are a young girl."

"But tell them!" sobbed Mina.

"Come with me." Mrs. Hoza led Mina to the officer. She said, with a certain rough dignity: "This girl asks me to tell you that she is going to be married the day after tomorrow." The officer said: "Indeed? That will be fortunate for her husband, whoever he is, *if* they are married the day after tomorrow." He was enjoying this little piece of badinage. "But permit me, Madam, to inquire exactly what leads you to believe that this very charming young lady is going to be married the day after tomorrow?"

"It is all arranged," said Mina, eagerly.

"So?" said the officer, with sympathy. "Arranged? Oh well, if it is *arranged* . . . of course, if it is *arranged* . . . we-ell . . ."

"Yes? Yes?"

"Why, then, this being the case, I will take an airplane at once and fly to Berlin, and speak to the Fuehrer. And I shall say to the Fuehrer: 'My Fuehrer, to my certain knowledge a very pretty young lady in Dudicka is going to be married the day after tomorrow. I would like you to do something about it.' And the Fuehrer, who, as you know, is tender-hearted and full of love, especially where you Slavs are concerned, the Fuehrer will immediately withdraw from Czechoslovakia and make your husband King, or at least President. Will that suit you?"

Mina burst into tears.

Mrs. Hoza said to him: "That was very funny. We are women, helpless, and you have had your joke with us. Now, as the wife of the Mayor of this village, I ask you what you intend to do with us?"

"Oh, as wife of the *Mayor!* Well . . ." the officer, tired of his joke, spoke brusquely: "You are to be taken away, that is all."

"Taken away? Where?"

"I do not know where, and I do not care where. It is an order. That is all."

"All of us?" said Mina.

"Every last one of you." A silence had fallen in the church. The officer's voice, although he had not raised it, seemed to boom like thunder. "We are going to demonstrate to you Slavs that Germans are not to be killed with impunity." Out of a horrible breathless quiet the voice of Etta Hertl said: "We have killed nobody."

"No, nobody ever does kill anybody."

Several German soldiers giggled.

Mrs. Hoza asked: "And our husbands?"

The officer paused before replying. He said, afterwards, that the indrawn breaths of the women created a draught, a positive suction: he was something of a raconteur and made a good story out of it which earned him many a drink in the company of fellow officers later on. He looked from face to face; noted great staring eyes, and in the dimness, black ovals and circles of open mouths filled with shadows. He savored this moment and then said, picking his words with the fussy hesitation of a gourmet picking out choice morsels in a salad: "I beg your pardon, but I did not quite catch that. Would you mind repeating?"

Fifty women exclaimed simultaneously: "Our husbands!"

(This, he told his friends, was like a high wind; and added an artistic touch about a woman ten yards away who had been eating an onion.)

Still speaking with nerve-racking deliberation, he said: "Since you ask me, I will tell you. It is not in my nature to refuse ladies anything, for I am a man of tender heart."

He lit a cigarette and inhaled a great mouthful of smoke and then he said:

"Your husbands are going to be shot, provided they are over the age of seventeen." There was another silence.

"Shot?" said one woman. "Shot?" said another. And twenty more said "Shot?"

"Shot," said the officer. And then he became afraid. There were nearly two hundred women in the church. They were all looking at him. One of them, a rawboned dark woman of fifty, came towards him, making strange rasping noises in her throat. He backed away, reached the door, said to the Sergeant and the soldiers: "Outside," speaking very rapidly. The officer, the Sergeant, and the soldiers got outside and slammed the heavy doors just as the dark woman reached them. She beat the wood with her fists, shouting threats without articulation. Other voices joined hers. For a few seconds there was a ferocious wolfish howling. Then the voice of Mrs. Hoza cried: "Be quiet!" The voices died away, and Mrs. Hoza was heard to say: "I think we had better pray."

Outside, the officer mopped his forehead with a handkerchief and said: "There is no holding women when they get that way. I want a double guard at every door and window. If any woman so much as puts her nose outside, shoot to kill."

But in the church the women were praying. Only Etta Hertl sat still staring in front of her, still clasping to her large bosom the little girl, Maria. The rest of them made the air of the church shake with frightful supplications.

Mrs. Hoza looked into Etta's eyes. Etta closed hers for a second, and her body seemed to twitch.

Then she recovered herself and said: "My baby is kicking."

"What is to become of him?" cried Mrs. Hoza, looking up to the black ceiling which lay between her and the sky.

But the sky gave no answer.

* * * * *

The officer exchanged a little conversation with a Captain. The Captain said: "I dare say there is some good stuff in there?"

"Nothing much. A few kids that might be usable. There are scarcely a dozen or fifteen fit for officers' brothels. And for that matter, not an enormous number good enough even for the common houses. Most of them are real peasants, plain and mousy or dark and hairy as bears."

"I don't mind a nice firm peasant girl," said the Captain.

"Well, every man to his taste, but I prefer something rather more sophisticated . . . something that knows what to do, and how and when."

"Yes, that's all right, but for general purposes there's a hell of a lot to be said for one of those healthy, big-bottomed farm-wenches."

"Personally, I prefer refinements, certain refinements, which an uneducated woman finds difficult to understand. Anyway, there are plenty of women."

The Captain said: "They go from fifteen years old upwards in there, I think?"

"Well, I didn't count their teeth."

"And the kids?"

"Oh, Neuberger is in charge of those, and I don't envy him."

The Captain said: "Oh, I don't think Neuberger will mind very much." He grinned.

"Oh-oh."

Fists hammered the inside of the locked door of the church, and a woman's voice screamed: "Sir! For the love of God! She said that our children were not coming with us! Sir! Dear, kind sir, she's telling lies! Tell her she's telling lies! She always was a liar! Officer! Mister! Gentlemen! Your Excellency, my lord! Sir!"

The young officer winked at the Captain, and cried: "Yes?"

"Are our children coming with us? They are, aren't they?"

"Your what?"

"Our children! My Otmar! My Lili!"

"No, I'm not your Otmar!"

"No, sir, please . . . gentleman, you are sending us away . . . aren't we going to take our children, my Otmar, with us? We are, aren't we? Say yes! Please, sir, say yes!"

"Watch this!" said the young officer to the other.

The Captain growled: "Ah, leave the poor cows alone!"

"No, but just listen . . ." the young officer shouted: "Do you want me to say yes?"

A broken voice cried: "Yes!"

"Say please, then."

"Oh . . . please, please, *please*, PLEASE!"

"Well, if you want me to say yes I say . . . Yes!"

A sob of relief; and a cry of: "I told you so!"

The Captain then continued: "I say yes in order to oblige you, as a gentleman to a lady. But if you want to know the real truth—*No!* Your children are *not* going with you!"

"Oh, leave the miserable bitches alone," said the Captain, as the women cried out in agony.

"Why, since when were you sentimental about Slavs?"

"True . . . they are not German women . . ." said the Captain, as one who sees a point. He added: "Still, they've got enough. Let 'em alone."

The same woman's voice sobbed: "What is going to become of them?"

And the young officer replied: "They will be in better hands than yours."

XVI

Shades of the Prison-House

THE WOMAN who had cried out to the officer was
Marta Lalak. She had a son named Otmar, and a
daughter nicknamed Lili. Her husband was a timber feller, a simple-minded man known as "Smiler."
They had celebrated Otmar's twelfth birthday only
a week before. Smiler Lalak, who liked carving
things out of wood, had made the boy a boat. It was
a cross between a yacht and a galleon; a boat of no
known kind, in the front of which there was a little
figurehead carved in the shape of a draped woman.
The Smiler had done a wicked thing; the boat
needed two sails, and he had cut one out of the tail
of his only sound shirt and another out of the bottom edge of Marta's second shift. Thus, the boat
sailed. He took Otmar and Lili to the stream, and
they launched it with a great uproar, naming it *The
Lili-Otmar*. The Smiler's ideas about boats were a

little confused: the *Lili-Otmar* floated lopsidedly.
All the same, it floated. Later, when Marta, infuri-
ated, accused him of ruining good linen—the last
linen they were ever likely to possess—the Smiler
grinned sheepishly and said: "What the devil! Nobody sees the tail of a shirt, and nobody sees you
in your shift, except me, and I don't mind. Let the
boy have a boat. We are only young once, and in
my time it was different: there was more pleasure in
life." Then, seeing that Lili was looking at the boat
with round, melancholy eyes, he started at once to
make her a doll with a movable head and jointed
limbs, and being, in spite of his slow movements and
massive bulk, a man who was very quick and dex-
terous with his fingers, he finished the doll in four
days. It was a large and handsome doll with a remarkably fine head of light hair—real hair. Where
had the Smiler got the hair? Off his own head. One
side of his scalp was almost bald where he had
clipped it. And where had he found the spotted blue
silk out of which the doll's dress was made? Mr.
Hoza had something to say about that: a scarf which
his wife had washed and which had been hanging
out to dry had mysteriously disappeared. There was
a scene. The Smiler said: "If I gave the boy a present, I had to give the girl a present too. And could I
give her a naked doll? It would be indecent, it might
put bad ideas into her head. After all, Mr. Mayor,

[171]

she's only six years old." The Smiler was so good-humored and so obviously innocent of anything but the best intentions, that the Mayor simply said: "Go to the devil," and let the scarf go.

Lili wanted to call her doll Lili too. Otmar protested. It was not right that a doll should have the same name as a ship. So she called it Lotti. She told the doll stories, had long and confidential conversations with it, took it for walks, and punished it severely for acts of disobedience. To other little girls of her own age she would say: "Oh dear, I don't know what I've done to have borne such children," in imitation of her mother. She stuck little bits of pink flower petals on the doll's cheeks and wailed that Lotti had small-pox, and also a disease which she had invented, called "Striped Fever."

When the soldiers came that morning they had heard sounds of animated discussion in the garden of the Lalak house. The little girl was saying: "If only you would be good! I work my fingers to the bone for you, and what thanks do I get? None! You never listen when I talk to you! You disobey me! I lie awake all night crying my eyes out over you! I have a pain here, just here . . ." A giant rifleman, approaching on tiptoe, saw Lili pressing a hand against her thin chest, and pretending to cry, while the big wooden doll stared stupidly at her with its painted eyes. ". . . just here over my heart, my poor heart. Oh dear, what will become of you when you grow up, if you are already so naughty when you are a child?"

The rifleman said: "The doll cannot understand what you are saying to it." He was a practical man, it must be understood.

"She can!" said Lili.

The rifleman, who was prone to rationalist argument, said: "It is made of wood. How can wood understand?"

Lili replied, passionately: "She is not made of wood!"

"What, then, is she made of?"

Lili could find no answer to this, so she said: "You are made of wood! Another rifleman said:

"Hermann, the child is right . . . about your head, at least." Then he said to Lili: "You must come with us."

"I must go to school," said Lili.

"Yes, you are going to school." The second rifleman took her by the hand. She still clutched the doll. When they reached the street the doll's head-dress fell off; it was made of paper.

"Wait a minute, or Lotti will catch cold," said Lili. The rifleman paused while the child readjusted the paper cone on the doll's head. He had a child of his own somewhere in Darmstadt. "Oh, she catches cold, does she?"

"You don't know what trouble I have been having with her," said the child.

"Much trouble?"

"My hair is turning gray," said Lili. Then she added in a rush of confidence: "My father cut his own hair off to make hair for Lotti. And Mother called him names. But I didn't. I wish her hair was long enough to plait. But it's fashionable to have short hair, you know."

"Is it now?"

"But it is immoral to paint your face," said Lili.

"Ah, you're not far wrong there," said the soldier. "What's your name?"

"Friedrich Betzendorfer."

"Everybody calls me Lili. You can, too."

"Thank you."

"Why are you taking me to school?"

"You are going to have a holiday, little girl."

"Is Otmar coming too?"

"Yes, Otmar is coming too. He is coming along behind us with his boat."

"Is Father coming?"

"No."

"He said that if he could get hold of some wheels, he would make a little cart so that I could take Lotti for rides."

"Who is Lotti?"

"*This* is Lotti; I told you already." Then she asked:

"Where are we going for a holiday?"

"To a lovely place with lots of other children."

[174]

"For long?"

The soldier became angry. He said, roughly: "Oh, shut up!"

Lili was silent. She clutched her doll with all her strength. The soldier let go of her hand and fumbled in a pocket. He pulled out a piece of chocolate, thrust it into her hand, and said, more violently still: "Chocolate. Eat it, and don't ask questions."

"Why mustn't I ask questions?"

He did not answer. They reached the little schoolhouse. He pushed her gently. She went in. To her surprise, she saw that the schoolroom was crowded. There were boys and girls who were almost grown up, and others, not more than four years old, in relation to whom she herself felt big and strong and deeply experienced.

One thing horrified her. She did not know what it was. But it was this: they were all silent.

There were soldiers in the schoolroom, too. There was no sign of Mr. Marek, the schoolmaster. But by the blackboard a stranger stood—a big, upright man in a tight uniform, armed with a big pistol and shod with big boots. He had a dark face which was at the same time pale; a high and prominent forehead and black eyebrows beneath which large brown eyes gazed down in a peculiar fixed stare. Lili thought that he had a funny nose: it was flat at the bridge, and the point of it turned up a little so that she could see his thin nostrils. His upper lip bore an oddly in-

[175]

congruous mustache of the kind that the Fuehrer wore. It was incongruous because his mouth was like a woman's mouth—like the mouth of a shrewish, vindictive and angry woman. Beneath this soft and savage mouth there projected—incongruously again —a great bony chin.

When he spoke his voice was startling: it had an irritating, penetrative thinness. He said: "Are they all here?"

Somebody said: "Yes, Captain."

Captain Neuberger looked down. Every child was staring at him. He glanced from face to face, sometimes pausing for a moment, until he was looking at the faces by the door.

He pointed straight at Otmar Lalak, and said: "Come here!" Otmar put down his boat. Captain Neuberger said: "What is that you have there? Bring it here."

Otmar approached the blackboard. The Captain took the boat and looked at it. "And what is this supposed to be?" he asked.

"It is a boat, sir."

"A boat." Captain Neuberger laughed. Then he reached out with a large white hand, and took Otmar by the chin, tilting his face upward. The boy tried to look at him boldly. But there was something in the Captain's eyes that frightened him: they did not look, but stared; they had no expression, and they seemed to be a little too large for the eyelids.

[176]

They reminded Otmar of chestnuts bursting out of their outer coverings. "What is your name?"

"Otmar Lalak, sir."

"How old are you?"

"I shall be thirteen in eleven months and three weeks," said Otmar, proudly.

"What a big boy you are."

Otmar said nothing. He lowered his eyes.

The Captain went on: "Why, one of these days, before you know where you are, you'll be shaving, eh? But what a pity it would be to spoil that little face with a nasty bristly beard, eh? Eh? Wouldn't it, eh? And where did you get your fair hair, eh? From your father or your mother, eh?"

"My father, sir," stammered Otmar.

"And your skin from your mother, eh? Eh?"

Each time the Captain said *"Eh?"* the boy started.

The Captain smiled, uncovering large white teeth, and said: "Are you afraid of me? Eh? Are you? Eh?"

The boy Otmar said nothing. The Captain continued: "Do you think I'm going to eat you? Eh? Do you, Otmar?"

Two soldiers standing behind the Captain nudged each other.

"No, sir," said Otmar.

"Like a little apricot? Eh?"

"No, sir."

Then, in a husky and gentle voice the Captain said: "Don't be afraid. I'll look after you."

"My father looks after me, sir," said Otmar.

"I will look after you," said Captain Neuberger. "Wouldn't you like that?"

"No . . . no, sir."

Captain Neuberger knocked him down with a backhanded slap on the head. "Discipline," he said, very gently. "Discipline!" He hissed the word. "Get up, Otmar."

Otmar got up, and his face was bloodless as this paper.

"Now, Otmar, wouldn't you like me to look after you?"

"No, sir."

Captain Neuberger smiled and said: "I am afraid that it is going to be necessary to teach you the meaning of discipline."

With delicate motions of his big white hands, he turned back his cuffs.

Lili ran forward, crying, holding out her doll, and stammering: "I'll give you Lotti . . . but please don't hit him."

"Now . . ." said Captain Neuberger, smiling with a dreamy look on his face.

The rifleman called Friedrich Betzendorfer clenched his teeth and, in order not to see, looked at his boots.

XVII

The Trench

Joseph Lalak, the Smiler, was talking to Karel Marek, the schoolteacher. "I don't think there is anything much to worry about, Schoolmaster. It stands to reason, there can't really be," he said.

"Smiler by name, Smiler by nature," said the schoolmaster.

"My opinion is, that this is nothing but a job of forced labor."

"Do they send half an army with airplanes and tanks and God knows what to conscript a few men for a job of labor?" asked Elias, in his grumbling voice. "No, according to the questions they have been asking, I'd say that they were going to swing up the whole bloody lot of us on a tree, just as a sort of warning to the rest."

"They can't do that," said the Smiler.

"They can do anything," said the innkeeper. "And

why have they taken all the women away? And what was that horrible screaming? No, you mark my words, this is something big and serious. They have wiped out people before now."

The Smiler said: "But we haven't done anything."

"Had we ever done them any harm?" asked old Balaban. "Had we ever? Had I ever? No. But all the same see what they did to us."

"Well . . . let them leave Teresa alone, and I won't care," said Roman Kafka. "What a woman she is! What a woman! If she says she's going to have boys, she has boys."

Smiler Lalak, suddenly remembering something, said: "Roman, I remember seeing in your shop a little, just a silly little kind of square box."

"What do you mean, square box?"

"A kind of a little brown box, with a sort of carving on the lid; just a box."

"Well?"

"Well, it's like this, Roman; I made the little girl a sort of a doll, you see; and now I kind of promised to make her a little cart if I could get hold of a couple of wheels. You know what kids are, they like to wheel things up and down and play steam engines or fire engines, or the devil knows what-all. Well, Roman, it came into my mind that that silly little box would be just the thing."

"I'll see you in hell first," said Roman Kafka. And

then he seemed to feel that he had said something of a terrible hidden significance, for he stopped, his mouth open. Then he muttered: "Yes, you can have the box. You can have it by all means."

Lalak grinned from ear to ear and said: "I was working out the business of wheels. I noticed, Roman, that you have, as a sort of prop to your outhouse——"

An officer suddenly shouted: "Pay attention!"

Silence fell.

"How many of you here can handle a pick or a shovel?"

Most of the men could. The officer continued: "I want about twenty of you for a digging job. The youngest and strongest. Stand still, thin out there! Let me look at you."

Followed by two soldiers armed with Schmeissers, he strode around the room, pointing first to one man and then another. "You . . . You . . . You . . . how many is that? Twenty? Well, we'd better have half a dozen more. You . . ." He pointed to Roman Kafka; to Elias Svatek, and to Rudolf.

Rudolf, who had been standing very close to the Nazi guards, said: "Captain, for heaven's sake don't put me out there with them. Not if they have spades, or picks, especially not then. They'll kill me. They know I've helped you. I swear they'll kill me. Him, that one, Roman Kafka, he swore he'd kill me. They all hate me because I told the truth, because I told your captain. Don't send me out there with them, not with spades. I swear they'll kill me!" Sweat was running down his face. He talked rapidly: "The other officer, the other gentleman, he promised faithfully that I should be rewarded. I said to him: 'Do I deserve a reward, Captain?' and he said to me: 'You shall be rewarded,' that's what he said."

The officer looked at him and said: "Oh yes, you're the one, aren't you? Come on, you too."

Then Marek raised his voice and said: "Roman, remember, you are not to touch him! No man is to touch him! Remember that, my friends! Judas Iscariot must be left to God!"

"You can shut up and come outside with them," said the officer. "You talk too much. Come on, Slav!"

Marek, and twenty-five others, went out into the street. Dudicka already looked desolate. Men were tearing down the last bits of metal from the church roof. One of them was wrenching at a cross fixed to a gable-end. As Marek looked the cross came away and fell with a heavy ringing noise into the street, where another man picked it up and looked at it and then tossed it onto a heap of broken metal. A pioneer, with a great pair of pincers, was tearing the metal effigies of Christ from a number of wooden crucifixes. Others were throwing into a truck great shovelfuls of small articles of brass, candlesticks, lamps, trays, old kettles, ancient pots which were no longer usable but which had been kept polished because of their cheerful brightness. They had even torn off locks and handles of doors. Objects made of tin, or tinned iron, lay in a separate heap. Marek saw specks of strange color in this heap, and recognized the outlines and tints of cheap tin toys, trains and motor-cars and humming-tops which had cost a few pence each and which he had procured for the younger children the Christmas before. Next to all this lay a glittering mass of scythe blades, saws, knives, and sickles: tools of wrought iron and hammered steel, some of which had been treasured and kept sharp and bright for generations; for with these tools the people of Dudicka had cut their food and their shelter out of the earth, the rocks, and the forest. The last few cows and oxen lowed in an open truck; there were no more pigs to take away. He saw, also, that paper had not been forgotten. Something like a cold finger seemed to pluck a twanging string in his breast as he perceived the brown covers of schoolbooks, the green backs of geography textbooks, the orange-colored arithmetic books, the red spines of history primers, and many black prayer books—all inter-mingled with stacks of fluttering periodicals, cata-logs, newspapers, and letters. All the paper that existed in Dudicka was not nearly enough to fill the very smallest of the trucks.

[183]

More than a hundred soldiers stood about the group of diggers. In the street several companies of riflemen were standing in platoons.

The officer said: "Every man take a spade." He pointed to a stacked row of picks, spades, and shovels.

The men of Dudicka knew, then, that they were doomed. Leopold said: "I was going to be married the day after tomorrow," and tears ran down his cheeks into his youthful mustache.

"And Teresa?" said Roman Kalfa. "And Teresa? And——?"

"Spades!" said the officer. "File past one at a time, and each take one spade!"

They did so, walking like men in a dream.

"I don't understand," said Roman, "I don't understand. I don't see. What have we done? I don't understand."

* * * * *

"You will in a minute," said the officer. "File past one at a time. Each man take a spade. Move yourselves!"

He added: "And by the by, in case you want to try anything, let me remind you that there are fifty Schmeisser guns pointing at your guts."

They picked up the spades listlessly.

"March!"

They stopped in a field near the stream. The Smiler, with a forlorn smile, said: "This is where we launched Otmar's boat."

The field was known as "Lovers' Field." Many girls had been got with child there. At the western edge of the field the ground rose abruptly. The people of Dudicka called this part "The Bed." The officer pointed. A large rectangle had been marked with pegs.

"Dig here," he said. "You have precisely one hour." He looked at his watch. "And dig deep if you don't want the dogs to worry you."

The men said nothing. Grain by grain, like rice out of a torn sack, hope had dropped away. Now they felt empty.

An officer said to another: "Would *you* dig your own grave if you knew you were going to be shot in an hour's time?"

"I don't know. Say somebody said I'd be shot on the spot if I didn't? I'd dig, I dare say: while there's life there's hope. An hour can be a long time. Something might turn up. You never know. It can't, but you never *know*. Men have been reprieved before now, just before the fire order. Besides . . . everybody would rather have a grave than be left lying about."

The men of Dudicka dug into the soft soil. Spadefuls of black earth flew up, seemed to hang sus-

[185]

pended, and then fell with heavy slapping sounds.
Kobra worked with silent deliberation. Smiler Lalak
worked with care: he liked the labor of digging and
the feel of a spade biting the ground. The Balabans
grunted rhythmically. The trench grew deeper. The
soldiers watched. Some of them fidgeted nervously.

Then, suddenly, Marek paused and said:

"This will be our bed tonight, friends. Yes, tonight we must all sleep together and make our earth
richer by being a part of it. Our bodies must go to the
flowers and the grass, and our souls must go to God.
Dear friends, lift up your hearts! Seeds also are
thrown into the dirt when their time comes, but there
comes another season and then they rise again. Be
brave and hold your heads high, and ask God to give
you strength to die with dignity as men ought to die.
Brothers, our roads are nearing the sea. Have courage, for this is not the end! Our dead look on, my
brothers, our dead look on!"

"Silence!" said the commanding officer. "Dig!"

The men, who had paused to listen to Marek,
plunged their spades into the soil.

Then Marek paused again. He listened. Down the
calm air floated a new sound. It might have been a
crying of lost birds as it rose, thin and wretched,
above the noise of a starting engine; but it was the
heartbroken chorus of the children. The schoolmaster leaped out of the trench and stood, trembling.

[186]

"My children!" he cried. "You dogs, what are you doing to my children?"

"Get back there," said the officer, drawing his pistol.

The noise grew louder. The men stopped working and stood, panting. "Children! Children!" shouted Marek.

"Cover them!" yelled the officer. Soldiers made a ring round the trench. Fifty Schmeissers pointed down. "Blow the guts out of the first one that moves!"

An immense closed truck roared up the road. For a second or two the men heard the noise of a great weeping, ineffably hopeless. Then the truck accelerated, and was gone.

Marek turned in the direction of the road. He took one step forward. The officer shot him in the back. He fell on his knees. "Oh, sweet Jesus, my little children!" said Marek, and then lay still.

"Dig," said the officer, putting back his pistol. "You have nineteen minutes more."

XVIII

The Winding Cave

On that nightmarish journey two children died. They were the luckiest of all. The rest never recovered from the horror of it. Captain Neuberger had achieved a miracle of stowage. He had squeezed a hundred and fifty-six children into a space calculated to accommodate forty-five standing men. They were packed neatly, with their faces towards the back of the truck. They had to stand like this for seven hours while the great vehicle rumbled, jolting and swaying, up the battered road away from everything they knew and loved. Their little heads were knocked together like nuts in a bag. Many were sick. Soon, they began to suffer the torments of thirst, but the truck rushed on. A terrible close heat sucked the strength out of them. They cried with fear, pain, helplessness, and dread of the dark unknown, until they were too weak to cry any more. If Otmar Lalak survives the beastliness of the Approved School, where he is being taught how to be a slave, and if he lives a hundred years, he will still wake up sweating and screaming every night when he remembers that ride. He stood, aching and bleeding from his frightful beating, but tried to soothe Lili, who clung to him and sobbed. They had taken away her doll: they had said that there was no room for it. Catching the eye of Rifleman Betzendorfer, she cried: "You told me lies!" and she wrung her tiny hands as she looked at her brother, and writhed with the agonizing, impotent pity of a child, and said: "Poor Otmar, poor, poor Otmar, oh poor Otmar. . . ." over and over again. In the truck Otmar tried to hold off the boy in front of him so as to make more room for her. But this was impossible. He fainted once: there was not room for him to fall. Later, he tried to lift Lili and ease her legs; but he was sick and weak. Every touch sent needles of burning pain into his shoulders and buttocks. He remembers the sounds and the smells; and how the slits of light grew gray and then black. He will not forget how all of a sudden Lili became limp, silent, and heavy. She was dead. The truck roared up the road. The children, mad with panic, began to push and strike one another, struggling for air and space. At the end of time, in the middle of eternity, the truck stopped. The back opened. There was a rush of cold air. The children fought their way

out in a screaming crowd. Two more were trampled
to death. One girl broke her legs leaping out. A guard
said: "Pouah!" and held his nose against the miasma
that came out of the truck. A light flashed green. A
great train hooted and ground itself to a standstill.
There was bread and water and soup. Then another
door groaned and opened. They saw the black in-
terior of another truck, and tried to run away, howling with terror. Otmar ran madly in the darkness.
Somebody caught him, slapped his face, punched
him in the stomach and dragged him back. He was
thrown onto a wooden floor. The children were
screaming again. The door slammed. A chain rattled.
Steam hissed. The train jerked, heaved, and whistled.
The children were in a cattle-truck. The train gathered speed and carried them away.

*   *   *   *   *

Also striving against a timeless darkness, Max
and Anna stumbled through narrow caves that
twined and doubled, lightless and dank and empty.
Down through the earth came the remote thunder of
the falling walnut groves that crashed before the
saws and axes of the German foresters.

Duda crept after them, whimpering. The last
branch had burned itself out. There was one sheet of
paper left in Max's notebook. The cold and darkness

had crept into Anna's heart. She followed Max, gripping the tail of his coat. At last she said:

"Max, let us go back."

"No, Anna, we must try and find a way. If we go back, all this trouble will have been wasted. We've got to go on."

"Can we have a little light, only for a second?"

Max lit the last sheet of paper. "This is the end of our lights," he said. "There is nothing more to burn, and my lighter is empty." He hurried on, protecting the flame with a cupped hand. She followed him breathlessly. A huge shadow bobbed behind him. Then he stopped. "Look," he said. The flame was licking the last two inches of paper. In its fading light Anna saw a blank wall of rock. Here, in utter impassibility, the cave ended. "I was wrong," said Max heavily. "We must go back."

Anna nodded. The light went out. She could hear the crackle of the ashes. They went back. She said: "It must be evening soon. Then we can go through the woods."

"I'm sorry I led you so far for nothing," said Max.

"I would follow you anywhere, just for the sake of following you. As long as you are with me it is not for nothing," said Anna. "I don't even mind the dark."

"You must be thirsty."

"Not very."

"And hungry."

"No, my love, I am full of better things than food."

They reached the cave of echoes, and the cavern that sparkled. Only it did not sparkle now, because the light was fading in the sky.

The last walnut tree fell.

Max, crouching at the entrance to the cave, peered out. A great gray twilight had fallen on the world, and with it a silence. They crept out, into the forest. But when they had passed the hillock, Duda grasped their hands, and dragged them into a clump of bushes. "Down!" he said, and seemed to dissolve. Max and Anna lay still. A long time afterwards, as it seemed, they heard footsteps. Heavy boots crunched the fallen twigs. A tired voice said, in Saxon German:

"Let's have a quick smoke."

A Berlin accent replied: "Make it a quick one."

A match scratched. Max and Anna caught the tang of cigarette smoke.

"Aaah," said the Saxon. Max saw him: he had seated himself on the ground. A thickset back placed itself next to his. "Well . . . I made my report. I saw Horner himself. Ever see Horner?"

"From a distance, once. All right?"

"Little fellow. Glasses. Looks as if butter wouldn't melt in his mouth. Funny, eh?"

"Were you in time for the shooting?"

Eh? The shooting? Yes, I saw it."

"Anything happen?"

*   *   *   *   *

The Saxon grunted. Then he laughed. "There was one skinny bloke who'd given information or something. It seems that Horner told him he'd be rewarded. This is funny. They had a mob of the Slavs digging a grave. See? They dug like hell. They dug like steam shovels. Funny, isn't it? They always do. The way I look at it——"

"This skinny bloke . . ."

"Well, they'd caught this skinny bloke in bed with somebody or other's wife. And do you know what she did afterwards? Cut her throat. By the way, any news from home?"

"Not a thing. Go on."

"I haven't had a letter for weeks and weeks. It makes you think. Christ, if I thought my old woman was carrying on with anybody while I was away, I'd . . . No, my old woman's straight as a die, dead straight. In fact it's just the other way with her—it's a full-time job getting her to sort of liven up at all. Well, there it is."

[193]

"Did I tell you what happened once with me and an officer's wife in Hamburg?"

"As I was saying, there was this thin bloke, and he'd been promised a reward for information, or something. Well, after they dug the hole, this thin bloke gets up, shaking like a leaf, and says: 'Sir, sir, you're not going to shoot me, not *me?*' And the officer says: 'No.' Then this thin bloke starts laughing and crying like a woman, and saying: 'Thank you, thank you.' And then the officer says: 'We're not going to shoot you, my friend. We're going to hang you for wasting our time with useless information and for lying.' And this thin bloke stands, like a monument, stiff, with his mouth open like a sack. And they tie his hands, and he turns round to the others and starts crying and says: 'Forgive me, forgive me!' And one of them, a big bloke, starts to laugh and laugh—and this big bloke is this thin bloke's brother! What do you think of that? Then they led up all the rest of the men. They packed the kids off in a truck, I hear, and all the women are to go to camps."

"And did they hang him?"

"On a bit of telegraph wire on a tree. I'd rather be shot than hung, wouldn't you?"

"I'd rather die of old age."

"Would you? I wouldn't. I had an aunt who died of old age. Couldn't do a thing for herself. She lived with us for a bit. Horrible. Ninety-nine. There was a rumor that she had money. All lies."

"Women any good down there?"

"The usual. All women are pretty much alike. Hear the shooting?"

"How could I hear the shooting with trees falling down all round me? God, we did a job! Those walnuts are hell. God knows how many we had on the job. Oh—did you know Steinke?"

"Wolfgang Steinke, you mean? I know a Wolfgang Steinke. Why?"

"Got caught under a tree."

"Dead?"

"Dead? He looked as if he'd been run over by a train."

"Ah, pity. I knew him a bit. 'Active Service,' eh?"

"Hm. Well, anything else?"

"One of the firing-squad blokes spewed his heart up."

"It takes some like that. How many did they shoot?"

"Oh . . . a hundred-and-something. Everybody from seventeen upwards. When *Horner* does a job, Horner does a *job*."

"I'd hate to be in Horner's bad books."

"They say even the Fuehrer's scared of Horner."

"I wouldn't like to be in a firing-squad."

"Well, they get the rest of the day free."

[195]

"I don't know, I just don't care much for it. What was it all about?"

"Well, these geezers are supposed to have killed von Bertsch or something."

"And did they?"

"How should I know? Firing-squads . . . The Slavs didn't take it too badly, all-in-all. Well, roll on Duration! I wish this war was over. I want a rest."

"Russia's just about down and out, I hear. So is England."

"What d'you think we'll do to Winston Churchill?"

"That little Jew-boy? String him up."

"You should've heard that thin bloke yelp! 'Mercy! Mercy!' Ha. Oh yes, and there was another bit of nonsense too. When the truckload of kids was going past, one old geezer drops his shovel and starts running after it. So the officer outs with the old Luger and lets him have it right between the shoulders. Bip!—Ah down he goes."

"What did he want to go and run after the children for?"

"Crazy, I suppose. He was their schoolteacher. Well, we'd better shift."

The Saxon put a hand on the Berliner's shoulder and rose, laboriously. They walked away.

Anna looked at Max. His face was dead and his lips were gray. There was blood on his hands where his nails had cut into the palms. "I am going to die, too," he said.

But Anna, in a calm, strained voice, said: "No. He did not want us to. We have got to try and live."

"And fight," said Max. His voice seemed to come out of an emptiness. "He never hurt anybody. They have killed him."

They crept down, hand-in-hand. The evening star was shining over the forest.

"He loved everybody," said Anna.

"Everybody loved him," Max replied.

They could not say anything more for a long time. The forest grew darker. In the distance, on the road, two trucks began to mutter as their engines started to turn over.

Duda whimpered and tugged at Max's sleeve. Then he made an inarticulate noise and ran away.

A man shouted. A woman screamed.

XIX

Night is Falling

THEY WERE TAKING the women away.

One by one the women had stopped talking, until a sick and dreary quiet had fallen in the church. Even Mrs. Pliva was exhausted, and could say no more. Blind with weariness she sat beside Etta Hertl. Etta was weary, too. They were all tired to the verge of death; used up, burned to ashes, crushed to dust. The girl Maria slept, her head on Etta's knees. Mina Petera gazed down at her. Maria's hair hung loose and seemed to be part of the shadows. Some women clung together, but nobody spoke. The little mice that lived in the church came out and looked with bright black eyes at the women as they sat bowed in utter dejection. They were lonely, the women of Dudicka; lost in the absolute cold of despair.

Then a baby cried and awoke another, who cried with it, and Mrs. Pliva muttered: "If it weren't that some of you might want me, I'd die before I let them take me away."

"God bless you, you good woman," said Mrs. Hoza.

They heard the trucks coming.

The door opened and an officer said: "Get up and get out, every one of you."

They rose. Immense and grim the trucks stood against the sky. "In," said the officer. Soldiers stood about them. Mina Petera looked up and saw their faces, and it was she who screamed. She screamed with all her soul. The sound of it rang as in a dead wilderness. It was thrown back by the hollow distance. The officer made a gesture. Two soldiers picked her up and threw her into a truck. Etta Hertl climbed painfully after her, followed by the girl Maria and Mrs. Pliva. "Right back! Right back!" The women dragged themselves in. Those who were carrying babies handed them up to others in the trucks. The two trucks filled. The women were packed shoulder-to-shoulder, and the doors crashed shut. The engines trembled. The officer cried: "Away!" The wheels turned, and the trucks struggled up the road into the twilight, towards the west . . . over the crown of the hill, and down, down into the outer dark. On that road Etta Hertl's child was born. It lived. But where is it now? Where?

* * * * *

[199]

In the field by the stream soldiers were burying the dead, all the men of Dudicka. The great grave was nearly full. There lay Roman Kafka, with staring eyes and a little blood on his chin. Beside him Lalak the Smiler sprawled, still smiling, like a man who is dreaming of something beautiful. Mr. Hoza looked stern and angry; but young Leopold, lying across him, gazed upwards with an expression of anxious expectation. Kobra's face was hidden. Balaban's eyes were closed: he lay beside his three sons. Elias Svatek's dead mouth sneered. The innkeeper's face was puckered, as if he had died in the act of tasting something bitter. Otakar Blazek had been thrown into the grave. His face had relaxed, so that it was mildly inquiring and full of gentleness. His old father, in death, seemed to glare at heaven with defiant resolution. One boy, seventeen years old, had been crying; there were tears on his cheeks, but now his lips were smiling. Another had caught his lower lip between his teeth, steeling himself for the fusillade; and so he lay, his teeth shining in the dying light.

"Don't forget this one," said a soldier, and took Karel Marek by the feet. "Hup!"

Marek fell on Otakar Blazek. Nobody would be afraid to be alone in a house with such a corpse. His white face was full of kindness. The soldiers covered it with earth. The grave was filled. The men who had lived in Dudicka lay under a black hump in the Lovers' Field.

The soldiers rested on their spades and wiped their foreheads.

One of them said: "Do you know, I think this is almost a record?"

Nobody answered.

Out of the forest there came, faintly, the echo of a rifleshot.

"They've caught a stray one," said the soldier.

*   *   *   *   *

It was Duda. Fear had got him by the throat. He ran back to his cave. The creeping shadows filled him with a wild terror. He wanted to hide. He wanted to comfort himself with his poor madman's treasure of gaudy beads and colored glass: he was worried about this. Horror was everywhere. The forest was perfidious. There was a strange smell in the air. Duda ran, forgetting to be cautious. He ran like a stag, and reached the little hill. A soldier saw him, raised his rifle, took quick aim and snapped a shot at him. It was a lucky shot. The bullet hit Duda in the back of the head. He rolled down. The soldier went over and looked at him. Duda was lying on his back. His ragged and fantastic coat had opened. Clasped to his breast, tightly clutched in his left hand, was a china cat with blue eyes. As the soldier

looked, something appeared out of a rent in the lin-
ing of the coat. It was a young rabbit, stupefied with
fright. The soldier picked it up and knocked its head
against the heel of his boot; put its warm and tender
body in his pocket, and went away.

The cave was never discovered. Perhaps a thousand years from now, somebody will dig down and
find Duda's treasure; and, turning over the colored
beads and carefully-laid-out shards of bright crock-
ery, and Karel Marek's watch, he will wonder what
kind of people lived here, and why they did the
things that they did.

*   *   *   *   *

In the village, Colonel Petz and Saxson made their
reports to Heinz Horner.

"There is not a living Slav in Dudicka," said
Saxson.

Horner made notes. The other officers also came
in to report.

"All metal and livestock have been collected and
roughly sorted."

"The walnut trees are down, and trimmed. The
stream was too narrow to float them. They have been
dragged to the road. I beg to report a considerable
quantity of very fine walnut wood."

Heinz Horner polished his spectacles. He said,
with his prim and exact enunciation:

[202]

"Now the artillery may practice. I do not want one stone left standing upon another in this village. Gentlemen, we will go to the road and watch."

He put on his spectacles and blinked.

"Where Dudicka stood, there will be a blank place on the map," said Heinz Horner, and stood up. He went out. As if some hidden hand had pulled an invisible wire, a hundred soldiers clicked rigid, and a hundred hands swung up. Horner looked at his watch. "I believe that this will be the end of acts of terror in Czechoslovakia," he said, and snapped his watch shut.

The Mercedes-Benz purred up the road. It reached the crown of the hill. "Stop," said Horner. He looked out of the window. "Are all our men out?" he asked.

"All," said Petz.

"Now," said Horner.

With the noise of a thunderstorm, a fieldgun battery opened fire.

XX

The Fire and the Ashes

To MAX AND ANNA it seemed that the whole forest was roaring like a beast that was hungry. They heard the heavy roar of the battery and the sharp, barking bursts of the high-explosive shells. Then something muttered: a house was falling. The old inn seemed to hiccough and stagger; it reeled like a drunkard, vomited broken bricks, and started to come down. Through ragged holes in its walls fire began to glare, first red, then yellow, and then fierce white. As if the very air were Hitler's sycophant, a gentle and insistent wind blew from the east. The wooden parts of the inn blazed high and bright. The battery thundered on. Still the guns struck and recoiled. Heinz Horner, on his hill, stood with his staff and watched. When the first spout of flame shot up, he nodded. The sum was working out. The total was being marked down, underlined in red. "They are making good practice," he said. Flecks of red light danced on his round spectacles. *The devil's schoolteacher*, thought Petz; and even Saxson felt, in the pit of his stomach, a certain crawling coldness. "Now let us see what the bombers can do," said Horner, looking at his watch.

There was a minute of aching quiet after the battery ceased fire. But then the sky heaved and pulsated. Light bombers were coming over. Their engines made a hideous, ecstatic sound like gulping laughter. The village of Dudicka, which had appeared to sway in the light of its own burning, now seemed to leap and dance. Bombs fell. One hit Kafka's house and scattered it like a handful of gravel. Another fell on the dump of rusty iron, and above the uproar of the blitz there rose, for a few moments, a kind of crazy singing as jagged fragments of iron girders and abandoned boilers flew whirling over the rooftops.

"They are firing into the village," said Max. "Our only chance is to go eastward. We must try that."

Anna nodded, but said: "I am terribly tired."

"So am I."

"I didn't sleep all last night."

"Nor did I."

"I was thinking about you," said Anna.

"And I was thinking about you."

Anna stumbled and fell. Max tried to lift her, but he was weak with fatigue. They rested for a short time. Then Max said: "If we don't go on now, my dear, we never will go on. Can you try to go on?"

They got up. "It might be best," said Max, "to go back to Duda's cave and hide there until everybody has gone. They can't stay much longer. There will be nothing for them to stay for. Only can we find the place again in the dark?"

Anna shook her head, but the forest was so black, now, that he could not see her face.

"Whatever happens, we mustn't be caught," said Max.

"They'd shoot you. They'd kill you."

"It isn't that I mind. I'm thinking of what would happen to you. You heard what that soldier said? The women go to camps. Can you imagine what they'd do to you?"

"I can imagine," said Anna.

"It would be better for you to die. Better than that." A root tripped him. He fell, and struggled up again.

"Are you hurt, Max?"

"No, Anna."

"Do you know where we're going?"

"No." Max's voice shook. "I think, eastward."

"I hate the dark. We have been so long in the dark. Max, I'm so tired of the dark."

They went on. Max said: "Yes . . . there was a blind alley at the end of that madman's cave . . .

and then when we came out again, it was nearly night . . . and then it was night . . ."

"Look!" said Anna pointing. They had come to an open space. There was a great redness in the sky. "Dawn!"

"No," said Max, swallowing. "That is Dudicka, burning."

"I had lost count of time," said Anna. Then she stopped. "I can't go on any more now," she said, "my feet are all cut."

Max felt his heart bursting with pity. He replied: "Let us rest, then. Nobody can see us. By dawn they must have gone."

"How wonderfully soft the ground is," said Anna, sighing. "Will you put your arms round me?"

They lay still. Max thought that she had fallen asleep. But she said, abruptly: "No, I'm not sure that it would be better for me to die."

"Eh?"

"I'm not sure that it would be better for me to die than be taken to a camp . . . or whether they might take me. If it were only for myself, then yes, it would be better to die over and over again. But if you die you go into the ground, and your soul goes either to heaven or to hell. You can't do any more here. *They* want that. But if you are alive, and still have your soul, something can still be done . . . somehow . . . You can help one, hinder another; you can put heart into another prisoner; you can perhaps destroy something of theirs. There is always time to die. If people died when they were in trouble . . . there would never have been any people at all. How often have I heard *him* say that? Even when men were like animals, they fought to live. They do . . . those creatures over there . . . they will lie and cringe and crawl to gain their ends. Dying won't gain them. *He* said so, Father said so. I called him Father. He wasn't my father. He was better than my father. He was the best man in the world. What he said was right: 'Live, fight for the truth, and keep your spirit pure.' "

"You are right," said Max. "Only the hope against hope and the little spark of faith in the dark keeps alive anything that is good in the world."

"But for myself alone, Max, I would much rather die . . . because I love you with all my heart," said Anna. And then she fell asleep, and in a little while Max slept too.

* * * * *

The bombing had stopped. Dudicka was burning itself to the ground. Horner still looked down, thinking. He said: "Now, in a little while, this place will be laid flat. It will be a clear space. It will be ab-

solutely wiped out. This will be our reply to Czechoslovakia. Soon, the grass will grow over the place. In
the winter the snow will cover it up. The wind will
spread its ashes smooth as a running track. Dudicka
will have ceased to exist."

He smiled. Then he remembered something: "The
two that ran away. Were they found?"

Petz replied: "They could not have passed the
ring of soldiers. They must still be in the mâquis, or
perhaps in the woods just near it."

"All the worse for them," said Heinz Horner. He
looked at his watch. "Yes."

Out of the night, in the blackness which was the
wood, a dull red glow appeared. Then another, and
another. Fire crawled up at a hundred points in a
vast semicircle. The points of fire ran together. The
flaming curve crept inwards.

Saxson said, with enthusiasm: "This is something
the Czechs will speak of in whispers for a hundred
years to come."

Heinz Horner stared at him. "What hundred
years?" he asked. "Are you forgetting that we have
their children? In fifty years from now the Czechs
will forget that they ever were Czechs. They will forget everything, except that they are Slavs and slaves.
And this is necessary, for the German Empire must
be built to endure ten thousand years."

He said this like a schoolteacher explaining simple

arithmetic. Saxson was silent. The Dudicka woods were blazing.

*   *   *   *   *

Max and Anna awoke. Little terrified animals were running over them and past them. The forest was full of smoke and lurid light. Like a shaking gray carpet a mass of rats ran past, squeaking, followed by bounding rabbits. A weasel passed, undulating. "Fire!" said Max, "Fire!" The breeze was blowing it towards them. The forest crackled and snarled like a leopard. Max seized Anna's wrist, and ran. A scorching wind overtook them. They heard the rustle and crash of young trees falling. A white-hot wall appeared behind them. The fire ran fast. Anna fell. Max picked her up and dragged her on. He felt his hair smoldering. The flames were closing in. They reached the mâquis. The fire seemed to hesitate. The green wood resisted it, but only for a few seconds; then the fire sucked it down. Anna reeled and Max caught her, lifted her with insane strength, and carried her. They broke out of the woods. He staggered to the stream. The water was almost boiling, but they drank.

"I think they have all gone," said Max, when they had recovered a little. "Try, just once more, try to go on."

They crossed the stream. The village was still

burning brightly. The whole world seemed to lie dead of fire under a shroud of smoke. They skirted the south side of Dudicka and reached the road. They were dying of exhaustion, but they walked. Once, Max said: "We have escaped."

"Yes," said Anna.

The road was empty. They reached the bend. And four German soldiers stood before them, at a road-block; a corporal and three privates.

The corporal said: "What, my pretty ones! We were expecting you!" He shot Max through the heart, and tied Anna's hands behind her.

She cried: "No! No! I want to die, too!"

"What's your hurry?" asked the Corporal. "You'll die one of these days all right. Now . . . walk."

He led her up the road. The bitter smoke hid them.

XXI

The End That is Not An End

DAWN WAS BREAKING. Through dense drifts of woolly white smoke a great and angry sun began to rise.

Dudicka was burned out. The woods smoldered. Saxson said: "The show is over: the lights are being switched on."

"*Durch Nacht und Blut zur Licht*," said Petz jerkily. "Through night and blood to light."

Heinz Horner nodded and put his watch away.

"This," he said, "is a practical demonstration of the punitive expedition. The Slavs killed one German, the Obergruppenfuehrer and General of Police von Bertsch. They have paid with a village, an entire village. Every adult male in Dudicka is dead and buried. Every woman has been taken away to a camp. Every child has been removed and placed in the proper hands. The village has been blotted out

[212]

so that not a stone stands on another, and its woods have been burned to ashes. All this has been done in a single day and a night. It is finished. It stands to reason that this is the end of insubordination and terror in Czechoslovakia. The price we have marked on the ticket is too heavy for anybody to pay. Gentlemen, you have done good work."

Smoke floated over. The valley below was filled with it. The wind had fallen. The road was littered with the ruffled corpses of dead birds: they had fallen, suffocated.

Looking down, Horner felt that he stood above the clouds.

He took off his spectacles, shook out the folds of a fresh white handkerchief, and polished the round lenses.

An eager little man in uniform was riding towards him on a powerful motorcycle. They heard the thudding of the engine.

"Yes, this is the end of the Terror in Czechoslovakia," said Horner, quietly.

The rider passed. There was a stuttering bang and a thunder of acceleration.

Heinz Horner's spectacles slipped out of his hands and smashed on the road. His handkerchief fluttered down.

"Stop that man," said Horner, and sat down on

the running board of the car. His face was blue. "He has shot me," he said; and then he began to cry out in a high, thin voice.

THE END